The Adventures of Rinaldo

The Adventures of

AN ATLANTIC MONTHLY PRESS BOOK

LITTLE, BROWN & COMPANY

BOSTON TORONTO

RINALDO

BY

ISABELLA HOLT

WITH PICTURES

BY *Erik Blegvad*

LIBRARY OF CONGRESS CATALOG CARD NO. 59-5271

FIRST EDITION

ATLANTIC–LITTLE, BROWN BOOKS
ARE PUBLISHED BY
LITTLE, BROWN AND COMPANY
IN ASSOCIATION WITH
THE ATLANTIC MONTHLY PRESS

Published simultaneously in Canada
by Little, Brown & Company (Canada) Limited

PRINTED IN THE UNITED STATES OF AMERICA

To Bob

who was too young to meet Rinaldo when the others did

The Adventures of Rinaldo

I

On a biting wintry evening, some five hundred years ago, more or less, the famous knight Rinaldo di Paldo was riding through the forest in a contented frame of mind. Although the snow was sifting down his neck and clustering in his eyebrows, he knew he was not far from a snug little inn, the only one within thirty miles, where he meant to pass the night.

He had come through the wars with honor, with only a few wounds, which had healed clean and quickly, and best of all, with a little treasure of jewels (his share of the sack of the castle of Plotzen) which he had sewn into the waistband of his red flannel underdrawers.

Being a thrifty man and tired of blood, he had decided to hunt out a small castle for sale, to marry a pretty wife and raise a colony of children — in a word, to enjoy his prime as a sensible man ought. He would have been surprised if he had known how many adventures still lay ahead of him.

The lights of the inn came in sight. Rinaldo eased his tired legs in the stirrups. "You shall have a royal supper of oats, Wingfoot," he promised as he clattered into the stableyard.

But while the stableboy's hand was stretched out to take his bridle Rinaldo checked his horse. He had heard a raucous burst of singing from inside the inn.

"What guests are inside?" he asked.

"Only a band of soldiers, your worship, of a lower rank than yourself, going home after the signing of the Peace."

Rinaldo rode over to look through the window. He had fought in the army of the Emperor Sigismund, and Peace or no Peace, he did not choose to trust himself and his jewels to the company of the enemy.

He said abruptly, "Bring me out a cut from the roast and a round from the loaf, a measure of oats for my horse and a coil of rope, and I will be on my way."

"Your worship is welcome here," said the boy, staring. "It's a bitter night, and you'll find no shelter in the forest."

"Do as you're bid," said Rinaldo, and the boy ran.

He came back with a mug of wine and another of steaming soup, both of which Rinaldo drank while sitting in the saddle. Then Rinaldo hung the packet of bread and meat, the sack of oats, and the coil of rope from his saddlebow, and giving the boy a coin, he pushed out into the cold night.

He was sorry to miss a warm bed and breakfast, but the

singing had been in the language of his late enemies, and through the window he had glimpsed a dozen enemy uniforms. Now Rinaldo was a brave man, but a careful one. He did not want to be robbed of his treasure. Nor did he want Wingfoot, the great white war horse whom he loved like a brother, to fall into the hands of thieves. They both might better camp out in the snowy forest.

So they pushed on, feeling out the road. The underbrush snagged them, the branches let down loads of snow on them as they passed.

Finally Wingfoot stopped short, trembling. Rinaldo urged him on, but he would not move.

"You have some reason," Rinaldo said, and dismounted.

At his next step he slipped and slithered down a bank some eight or ten feet high. Wingfoot had halted at the very edge of a low cliff. But Rinaldo reached the bottom safely, and once down, he found he was sheltered from the wind.

Wingfoot put his feet together and slid nimbly down the slope. Then he stepped over to a little stream that was trickling out from under a rock, and began drinking in great drafts.

"I have seen worse camps," Rinaldo said.

He found himself in a clump of birch saplings. Clearing away the snow, he made a fire with his tinderbox. It lighted up the dark forest and the falling snow.

He fastened one end of his rope to a log, and then took a turn with the rope around the tips of several saplings, drawing them down into a fan-shaped shelter.

He cut branches of evergreen and wove them roughly through the ribs of his shelter. He unsaddled Wingfoot, who stood without being tethered, and gave him his supper of oats. He piled his arms and armor under cover, and sat down to eat his own supper.

Then he rolled himself in his cloak and went quietly to sleep. Through the night Wingfoot pawed and snorted, as he smelled wild beasts prowling in the darkness. But Rinaldo was on good terms with all animals, and he was willing to take his chance with the wolves and bears.

In the morning he cooked himself a porridge of oats in his battered but useful helmet, and sat thinking what to do next.

In this wild country the inns stood about a day's journey apart, and his twelve enemies were likely to reach the same inn he did the next night. He wished he were a day's

journey behind them. He decided to go back on his tracks. So he scrubbed the porridge out of his helmet, put it back on his head, and broke camp. Then he and Wingfoot proceeded toward the inn they had left the night before.

Soon he heard coming toward him a jolly chorus of soldier voices. "I must pass through them," thought Rinaldo, "without letting them start a quarrel."

He took off his helmet, trimmed it prettily with branches, and perched it on Wingfoot's head instead of on his own. He was wearing huge wide boots, in which he carried a secret supply of gold ducats. One of these he took off, and placed upside down on his head, so that the toe dangled in the air above his nose, and the lower end of his red flannels showed below his breeches.

Then he rode directly toward the enemy, who were huddling in a little group and planning mischief. As he rode he sang merrily. It was not a very good song, because he made it up as he went along, but it caught their attention.

Tirra-lirra-lirra,
To-whit, to-whit, to-whee.
Welcome, jolly springtime,
Tirra-lirra-lee.

The enemy soldiers stared. "Jolly springtime, indeed! The poor fellow is touched in the wits."

"His helmet is on his horse's head."

"What's on his own head? It wags like an elephant's trunk."

"That is my boot," Rinaldo explained courteously. He took it off, bowed deep, and put it back on, arranging the toe carefully over the left eye. "It is full of money," he added truthfully — but they did not believe him.

"Where are you going, brave sir?" asked a soldier, snickering behind his hand.

"Oh, back to my own country to buy an estate," Rinaldo said, rolling his eyes foolishly. "I was a captain in the wars, and I am carrying a king's ransom in gold and jewels. Tirra-lirra — do you smell the roses?" and he sniffed the frosty air.

The men laughed out loud. One of them said, "But, Captain, you are headed the wrong way. You are riding straight back to the battlefield."

"Oh, no," Rinaldo said earnestly. "My road lies this way. I am out gathering flowers for my May basket. Tirra-lirra-lee!" he warbled sweetly.

One of the men made a winding gesture to show that poor Rinaldo had wheels in his head. They told him he would find a field of daisies farther on, and rode away laughing loudly.

Rinaldo was now precisely where he wanted to be — behind the twelve enemy soldiers. He rode back to the first inn, where he spent a quiet night, and then proceeded toward the west, stopping at each inn one day behind the enemy band.

And as he rode, winter passed. Spring did come to the fields and forests, and in April he reached the pleasant little dukedom of Hesse-Boneyard.

But by this time he had collected a number of most unusual friends.

2

Wherever Rinaldo stopped for the night the villagers crowded around, for he and Wingfoot cut a handsome figure as they rode into town. Even in his war-stained garments, Rinaldo was every inch a knight, and Wingfoot was a magnificent white charger dappled with gray.

Rinaldo enjoyed telling about his exploits. Sometimes he would order Wingfoot fetched from the stable so that he could spur to and fro in the village square, acting out a rescue or an escape. He told how at the sack of Plotzen when he was wounded and left for dead, his friend Colonel Gorchy risked his own life by carrying Rinaldo on his shoulders out of the burning castle. Wingfoot enjoyed an audience; he proudly reared and pawed the ground.

After such an evening the innkeeper would say to Rinaldo, "I can't take money for your lodging. You brought me a whole month's business in one evening."

It occurred to the thrifty Rinaldo to make such an arrangement with the landlords in advance. By way of giving good value, he made his entertainment more and more diverting. Everyone was pleased, particularly Rinaldo, who saved the ducats and jewels with which he planned to buy a castle.

He loved Wingfoot and Wingfoot loved him. Rinaldo had power over animals of all kinds, even fierce creatures obeyed him, and he was skillful in teaching them tricks. When he was performing, strange animals often peered over the heads of his audience, and gradually a number of these attached themselves to him.

The first was only a red squirrel, whom he named Pr-rwitt. Pr-rwitt delighted to ride on Rinaldo's helmet or between Wingfoot's ears, or to scamper up Rinaldo's long boot from the ground, and people laughed to see the tiny creature flirting his tail under the nose of the huge war horse.

The next addition to the party was a pig named Edward. After seeing Rinaldo, Edward took a dislike to the sty where he had been born, and without anybody's permission he set off down the road at Wingfoot's heels.

Wingfoot naturally left the plump Edward far behind; but at the end of the day Edward came stumping in, footsore and dusty, to the innyard, and laid himself exhausted at Rinaldo's feet. He turned his snout trustingly upward, with an expression of purest love in his little pig eyes.

Rinaldo could not reject such devotion. He let Edward trot behind Wingfoot. As Edward grew thinner he learned to trot faster, and he would trot till he fell down rather than be left behind.

Edward became a real addition to the entertainment, for he was extremely clever. He learned to grunt for no and

squeal for yes, he counted by patting his hoof on the ground, and when Rinaldo said, "Bow to the prettiest girl in the village," Edward would trot over to some young woman and double his forelegs under him.

So it went on. Several dogs joined the party, whom Rinaldo taught to jump through hoops; and a bear cub, who learned to dance on his stumpy bowlegs. A beautiful stag named Arthur came along out of the forest, and though he never learned any tricks, he was most handsome as he paced along at Wingfoot's side. Rinaldo found he had picked up two monkeys, though how they came into that part of Europe they were never able to tell him.

News of Rinaldo's coming ran ahead of him from town to town. People offered money to see his animals, and if he had not been a knight he would gladly have taken it.

One morning a sharp-faced boy turned up, who asked if he might travel with the party and take up pennies in his cap. He also offered to run ahead and chalk up notices:

Coming! Rinaldo di Paldo and His Animals.
Admission One Penny.

This did not strike Rinaldo as a proper proceeding. None of the knights of his acquaintance gave entertainments for money. But the boy pointed out that the knights were mostly too stupid to train animals, rather than too proud.

So Rinaldo engaged the boy. His name was Gulielmus, but Rinaldo called him Gooly. He proved to be an excellent manager. He chalked up such enticing notices, with drawings of Wingfoot standing on his hind legs and Pr-rwitt perched on the end of his tail, that the crowds grew greater and the money rolled in by capfuls.

So by the time Rinaldo reached Hesse-Boneyard the whole capital city was in a ferment over him. Rinaldo pitched camp in the outskirts, and planned to give shows for several days.

On the very first day Rinaldo was honored by a visit from the Duke of Hesse-Boneyard with his courtiers. These were old and disagreeable-looking people, but their robes were gorgeous with velvet and fur. The duke himself had a face like an elderly fox, and the fur was worn away around the edges of his cuffs, but he was a famous duke, who could wear what he pleased. In honor of the court Rinaldo made Wingfoot leap and prance. Two thrushes who had recently joined the party came flying in, carrying a blue ribbon between their two beaks, and perched on Arthur's antlers. The lords and ladies cheered, and Rinaldo said to Gooly, "This will be a fine thing for our business."

"I'm not sure," said Gooly, scratching his chin. "They tell me the duke is very, very fond of money."

"So am I," Rinaldo said cheerfully.

Gooly said, "He peered into my cap, and his mouth fairly watered at the sight of the pennies. Let us steal quietly out of town after darkness falls."

"Rubbish," said Rinaldo.

"Well, if you won't follow my advice I will follow it myself, and run away home, for I have no desire to go to prison."

"Run then," Rinaldo said impatiently. "Here are your wages."

And he hired a young barefooted girl, who had been feeding nuts and carrots to the animals, to take in the pennies. She said her name was Daffodil.

Rinaldo was wrong and Gooly was right, for the next day while Rinaldo was counting pennies in his tent, there appeared the Lord High Sheriff of the duchy.

"What do you mean, sir," this dignitary demanded, "by giving entertainments in Hesse-Boneyard without a license?"

Rinaldo said quietly, "I did not know it was required."

"You were trying to evade His Grace's lawful tax on animal entertainments!"

"How can there be a tax, when there has never been an animal entertainment till now?"

"There is a tax, never fear," said the sheriff. "The council passed the law this very afternoon, and it amounts to one hundred per cent of your takings."

"What! All my gate receipts?" Rinaldo cried. "I will never pay such a tax."

"Very well," said the sheriff. "You may sit in prison till you change your mind." He raised his eyebrows unpleasantly, and signaled with his finger, and several men-at-arms at once surrounded Rinaldo.

Young Daffodil had been staring round-eyed. Rinaldo said to her, "Daffodil, will you see that Wingfoot is fed? You may as well turn the other animals loose, you won't be able to manage them. — And take care of my armor, till I come back."

"Yes, sir."

After thinking a minute Rinaldo added, "And my boots!" He hated to leave his boots with a stranger, for the toes were stuffed with gold ducats, but there was at least a chance that the girl might be honest, whereas he was reasonably sure that the Lord High Sheriff was not.

"Yes indeed, sir," Daffodil said, turning her clear blue eyes to meet his. He thought, "Even if she is not honest, I'd rather she got my money than the rascally old duke." And off he went to prison.

He expected to be set free in a day or two, after paying some reasonable tax. But when he looked into the duke's foxy old eyes he realized how wise Gooly had been to run away.

When he told the duke he would not pay a hundred per cent tax, the duke replied with a nasty smile, "Perhaps a year in my dungeons will bring you to a more generous frame of mind."

Rinaldo sat gloomily pondering on the narrow bunk in his dungeon. It was true that sewed into the waistband of his red flannel underdrawers were jewels enough to pay the fine a hundred times over. But he had another use for those jewels. And if the duke found out about them he would pass some law which would let him confiscate them all.

Rinaldo fingered the hard lumps at his waistline, and concluded, like a good soldier, to make himself as comfortable as possible and to wait for what turned up.

For a whole month only his training as an old campaigner kept his courage up. He had no blanket in the stone cell except his soldier's cloak. He slept on a hard board. Twice a day the jailer brought him a hard crust of bread and some greasy lukewarm broth. Whenever he went to sleep he heard rats scurrying for crumbs across the damp stone floor.

To keep his health and vigor he did gymnastics and acrobatic tricks — juggling his gruel basin, or walking on his hands. And since rats were his only callers, he entertained himself with them. He coaxed the rats to come asking him for crumbs, and it was not long before he had trained them to sit up and beg, to dance in circles, to parade by twos and fours, and to roll over when he whistled. He passed hours every day with the rats, and they brought their friends and relations till he had no crumbs left for himself.

The jailer spent hours peering through the slit in the

door of the cell. He too brought his friends and relations, as well as plenty of extra bread crusts, so Rinaldo's dungeon was the most popular spot in the castle.

One fine day along came the duke in his moth-eaten fur robe and observed a jostling of shoulders around the door of the cell. People were shouting, "Move over, you've had your turn." . . . "I have not."

"What ho!" the duke shouted in his rasping voice, and the jailer's friends scurried away like so many mice. He put his long nose to the peephole.

Rinaldo unkindly led his performers into a corner which could not be seen from the door. The old duke shuffled away, and Rinaldo laughed as he heard him go.

Next morning came a page, who commanded Rinaldo to bring his pets to the banquet hall.

Rinaldo had half a mind to refuse. But any change was a change for the better, so he whistled his little rat-army together.

When he whistled, they came streaming out of the crevices. He marshaled them two by two, and whistled a jig, and the parade wound its way across a great open courtyard.

Through the arched gateway Rinaldo could see, far below, the farms and villages of the countryside like so many toys in a sandbox. But the lower half of the archway was closed by a huge, spiked wooden gate. It reminded Rinaldo that he was a prisoner. But he marched in soldierly style at the head of the parade, climbed the steps and made his entry into the great hall.

The duke was at dinner with his lords and ladies, who clapped their hands as the procession wound in. Rinaldo bowed as if he had been a duke himself, and then set his rats to marching and countermarching.

At first they were confused by the banquet hall, so much larger than Rinaldo's cell, and by the delicious smells of food. But Rinaldo fastened a bit of cheese to the tip of a long wand, and the rats ran after the wand. He hoped that he himself would be asked to sit down to dinner after the entertainment, for he was as hungry as the rats were.

The courtiers had forgotten all about dinner. They were leaning over one another to watch the wonderful show.

Suddenly noises broke out in the courtyard — "Whoa there! — Get back! — Help, whoa there, help!" There was a thunderous clatter on the entrance stairs.

Everyone leaped up, and stared at the doorway. The rats, losing their presence of mind, ran scampering under the ladies' wide skirts. So the ladies did some scampering and shrieking of their own, and climbed on top of the tables.

Wingfoot appeared in the doorway. His forefoot was lifted impatiently, his eyes were searching the dim hall. Rinaldo had never seen a creature so beautiful and proud.

The horse whinnied delightedly and crossed to Rinaldo's side.

"Well," said Rinaldo, "since you got in, you must have some means of getting out." So he vaulted into the saddle, made a courteous bow to the duke, and rode clattering toward the entrance.

"Stop him!" screamed the duke. But the armed guards had not been taught how to capture a large, determined war horse in a roomful of ladies. When they reached for Wingfoot's bridle he reared threateningly, and they slunk back from his hoofs.

Without hurrying, Wingfoot picked his way down the steps and out into the courtyard. The guards ran after him, fitting arrows to their bows.

"What next?" Rinaldo thought — for the spiked gate stood bolted as it always did.

All at once Wingfoot gathered himself like a steel spring, and launched galloping, straight for the gate. The spikes were fully seven feet high, and the opening in the archway above was not more than four feet higher. Through that small semicircle Wingfoot had leaped in, and that was the way he proposed to leap out.

Rinaldo crouched on Wingfoot's neck. The grand creature lengthened out in a flying leap. The stone arch brushed Wingfoot's ears and Rinaldo's hair. The rear hoof gave one click on the top spike of the gate.

But they were free — free, and racing down the slope, with the guards shouting helplessly behind them, and the arrows whistling past their ears.

3

Wingfoot galloped faster than any pursuer could follow, and carried Rinaldo away from the city of Hesse-Boneyard where he had met such bad fortune.

The sky was blue, the cherry blossoms looked like lace petticoats on the hillsides. Rinaldo had lost his circus, his armor, his boots and his ducats. But he had saved the jewels in his waistband, and thanks to Wingfoot he had his freedom. So, happy as a lark, he followed the road through the Boneyard Mountains.

Wingfoot was capering, more like a colt than a hard-working war horse. "Gently, my lad," Rinaldo protested. "Stop dancing on your toes." But Wingfoot kept on prancing with impatience.

They passed a boundary stone that marked the end of the old duke's land. A few minutes later Wingfoot turned aside into a faint path among the trees.

They were following a brook which widened out into a

pool, with a grassy glade around it. A fire had been built there, and the smoke rose fragrant through the trees, but no one was in sight.

Wingfoot sent out a long, imperious neigh. Rinaldo waited, but there was no answer, so he decided to take a much-needed bath.

He stripped off his clothes, which smelled of the dank dungeon, and then he splashed and snorted and tumbled like a porpoise till he was clean of prison filth and prison misery.

He regretted his lost circus. By this time the girl Daffodil, for all she looked so honest, was probably counting his ducats into the family sock.

Wingfoot was fidgeting and fretting, almost as if he wanted to get Rinaldo out of the pool. Suddenly he pricked up his ears, and trotted off into the farther woods.

Having enjoyed his swim, Rinaldo sat down on a rock and began giving his faithful red underwear a scrub. He washed it, thumped it, squeezed it, rinsed it and spread it in the sun to dry.

He was so cheerful over his laundry work that he noticed nothing till a branch snapped near at hand. He snatched up his army cloak to cover himself, for he was naked as a scaled fish.

However this was not an attack; it was a remarkable procession winding its way into the glade. At its head marched Edward the pig. Behind him came the performing dogs, with hoops in their mouths; then Chico the bear, waddling along like a drum major on his hind legs; then an assortment of everything from rabbits to monkeys; and Arthur the stag, who had brought along a doe and a

fawn. And winding up the parade came the grand white Wingfoot, with the two thrushes riding on his ears and Pr-rwitt perched on his tail, and the girl Daffodil in the saddle.

"Am I in prison and dreaming?" Rinaldo asked himself.

Daffodil's hair stood out around her head like a sunflower. Her waist bent easily to Wingfoot's stride. She was oddly dressed: her striped petticoat was flouncing high above her knees, and she was wearing Rinaldo's enormous boots, which were so much too large and long that she had tied them with string to her belt to keep them on. She carried Rinaldo's helmet and weapons on the pommel of the saddle.

Edward spied Rinaldo and broke into a clumsy gallop. All the animals broke ranks to welcome him. Soft muzzles pressed against his hands; moist velvety tongues licked his bare ankles.

"Here's your circus," Daffodil said, her face glowing

proudly as she looked at him over the heads of the animals.

"How did you manage them all?" he demanded in amazement.

"Oh, we lived together in the woods." She untied the strings and let Rinaldo's boots drop from her slim bare feet. "You will find your ducats safe, all but one that I had to spend for grain." She dismounted, and smoothed down her petticoats.

For once Rinaldo forgot his thrift. "Hold out your apron," he said, and picking up one of his boots, he emptied a stream of ducats into it.

"Oh no, sir, I don't want a reward." She dropped the corners of the apron, and the ducats rolled twenty ways into the deep grass.

"Don't be silly," Rinaldo said. He could give ducats away, but he could not bear to throw them away. "Pick them up like a sensible girl. You've given me back my circus, my armor and my gold. The ducats will be a dowry for you when you marry some fine young fellow in Hesse-Boneyard."

"But I am not going back to Hesse-Boneyard. The High Sheriff would clap me into jail for escaping with your property."

Rinaldo rubbed his chin. It was true that the girl's loyalty to him had made trouble for her.

He said remorsefully, "I must take you to the next town, and find you lodging with some motherly dame."

Daffodil put her arm across Wingfoot's neck, and the great horse nuzzled her ear. "I am handy with beasts," she suggested.

"You've proved that," Rinaldo said cordially.

Daffodil stared at him with her round, sky-blue eyes and asked, "Wouldn't I do you just as well as that coward Gooly?"

"Three times as well — if you were a boy."

"I'm not to blame for not being a boy. I want to go with you."

"Impossible!" said Rinaldo. "Young girls sit on window seats and do embroidery. I sleep in my cloak, and drink water out of a brook."

"I've never liked embroidery," Daffodil said with courteous firmness.

Not knowing what else to do with her, Rinaldo finally agreed that she was to travel with the circus till he could find her a pleasant home in some village.

"Now I must go and dress," Rinaldo said, as he gathered up his laundry.

"Good heavens, what holes!" cried Daffodil. "Come, let me have them, I'll put on a patch."

She took out thread and needle from a little pouch at her belt. With her pocketknife she slit off a corner of her own striped petticoat, and she began patching the red flannel underdrawers.

"There! Could Gooly have sewn as neat a patch?" she

demanded, flaunting the gaudy garment. "—But gracious, sir, what are these rocks in the waistband?" and she began to slit it open.

Quickly he stopped her. "Those are magic beads. I always wear them to keep off danger."

"You might let me see them," she said, pouting a little.

"Why, so I will," he cried. "I can trust you."

He shook out the jewels one by one and tossed them into her lap.

"Sir!" she cried, with her eyes as round as gooseberries.

"This is my share from the sack of Plotzen. When the castle was set afire I was left for dead, but Colonel Gorchy carried me out through the fire on his shoulders. Then when they divided the spoil, Gorchy stood up for my rights and made them deal me my share. After my wound was dressed he put the jewels into my hands."

"It was a noble action," said Daffodil, fingering the big diamond star.

"So I owe my life and my fortune half to Gorchy and half to you," he said warmly.

"Anybody would have done as much as I did."

"No," Rinaldo said. "Few would have had the honesty, and even fewer would have had the skill."

Daffodil played with the jewels, which shot out blinding sparks of color. The necklace was the collar of some knightly order, with a Maltese cross that was a rainbow of jewels.

"Try it on," Rinaldo suggested. "I shall never wear it. I mean to sell the jewels, and buy an estate, and found a family."

"But, sir," Daffodil asked, balancing the collar in her palm, "a knight like you — have you no castle of your own?"

"My father had a castle in Lombardy," said Rinaldo laughing, "but six of my brothers are living in it. I find it a trifle crowded."

"Why do you want a castle at all? This life is more fun."

"One gets tired of rambling," Rinaldo said, stretched at ease upon the grass. "I am thirty years old, and I have been a soldier for thirteen years."

Daffodil had just begun her rambling life, and she liked it very well. She went on playing with the jewels.

One was a six-pointed star, paved with small diamonds. At the tips were diamonds as big as peas, and in the center a great ruby. "You may have that one," Rinaldo said.

"It's too bright," Daffodil said, tossing it aside. "I like this better." She held up a ring set with two lustrous pearls.

"It was made for some princess," Rinaldo said. He slid it on her first finger. "Do keep it," he urged her, "in memory of how you saved my circus."

"Thank you, sir," she said gravely. In silence she sewed the other jewels back into their hiding place.

"Now be a good child and pick up the ducats you scattered out of your apron." And he went away into the woods to dress himself.

When he came back she was on her hands and knees, half crying, with only three or four ducats in her hand. "How could I have been so reckless?" she lamented.

"Don't cry." Rinaldo took a fagot from the fire, and touched the long grass to flame. When a little circle had been burned bare, he trod out the fire. There among the cinders lay the ducats, like a dewfall of gold.

4

Next morning Rinaldo opened his eyes to see not dungeon walls, but green branches and blue sky. He smelt a fragrance of sizzling bacon, and turning on his elbow, he saw Daffodil in her striped petticoat, crouching beside the campfire.

"Where in the world did you get the frying pan?" he asked.

She told him that before leaving Hesse-Boneyard she had gone back to her own house and brought away her big Flemish dog Bonzo. Bonzo had no circus talents, but he had been trained to pull a little cart. Into this cart she had loaded blankets, clothes and cooking pots. Bonzo trotted stolidly behind the line of march, and at night she used his shaggy shoulder for a pillow.

While Rinaldo was enjoying his good breakfast she made a tour of the beasts, taking burrs out of the lambs' fleece and thorns out of the dogs' paws.

"Do sit down," Rinaldo said. "You're spoiling my animals. You mustn't play nursemaid to them."

Daffodil kept on tidying up, folding her blankets, loading her cart. "You'll be worn out," Rinaldo said. "You have miles to walk today."

"Oh," said Daffodil, laughing, "I don't walk. You'll see."

She lifted her hand, and Arthur the stag came to her. He bent his stately head, and grasping his antlers, Daffodil launched herself sidewise upon his shoulders, where she sat with her face peeping out through the antlers as if she had climbed a tree.

"I'll be off ahead of you," she said. "I must reach the village of Unterberg by noon, to chalk up signs about the circus."

"You are worth eighteen of Gooly," Rinaldo cried — a compliment which pleased Daffodil greatly as she rode away.

Rinaldo put out the campfire, whistled the animals into line, and mounted Wingfoot. Edward led the line of march, and Bonzo's little cart came bumping along in the rear. Rinaldo scoured ahead to find the road Arthur and Daffodil had taken.

They came to a rocky glen with a bridge, and beyond the bridge an unmarked fork in the road. Rinaldo dismounted to look for Arthur's tracks, and found them running like a line of ditto marks. He was going to remount when through the humming woodland stillness he heard wild shrieks, rolling of heavy wheels, jingling of harness and pounding of hoofs.

These sounds came from a road which rounded a low cliff and sloped down to the bridge. Around the corner a great gilded coach came swaying, with the coachman tugging at the reins and the footmen clinging for dear life behind.

The four horses were running away. Their heads were stretched out low, and foam flew from their bits.

A lady was at the coach window, screaming with terror. She was trying to open the door and leap out, but the door would not budge.

Without thinking twice, Rinaldo leaped to the bridles of the runaway horses, and clung there, in spite of the hoofs which threatened to break his bones. The lead horses staggered to a stop. The coach lurched, but it did not overturn.

The footmen scrambled down and lowered the coach steps, and out climbed a young lady who, in spite of the battering she had received, had a fetching and elegant air.

Her skirt was of cloth-of-gold, and she managed it with soft, jeweled hands. She came swaying down the steps to Rinaldo, and flung her arms around his neck. She smelt like the sweetest flowers. "You have saved my life," she cried in a silvery voice. "How can I thank you?"

Rinaldo said, "You are thanking me very nicely. May I ask your name?"

"I am the Countess de Goldilocks, and I live in Castle Goldknob, around the corner of the mountain. You must drive there with me. I'll give you a new cloak and doublet for the ones you have torn in rescuing me, and you shall stay as long as you like."

"Delightful," he said, forgetting that Daffodil was already chalking up notices of his performance in Unterberg that evening. He was tired and shaken, and he found it pleasant to sink into the cushions of the coach, and to hold the velvety fingers of the Countess de Goldilocks.

They heard a horse coming along at a light, rapid trot. "Oh," said the countess, "that will be Count Considine." And looking into a pocket mirror, she arranged her curls.

Around the bend appeared a brilliant figure. He was riding a cream-colored horse with an ivory mane, his trappings were like jewelers' work. The count wore a yellow doublet slashed with violet satin. From his belt swung a dainty sword. His short russet cape matched the chestnut curls on his shoulders.

"Dear me!" Rinaldo thought disrespectfully. "What a side show Count Considine would make for my circus."

The count slipped gracefully from his horse, and clasped the countess's soft hand with his still softer one. "My pearl!" he exclaimed. "Thank heaven you are not injured."

"Small thanks to you," the lady said pointedly. "It was

this gentleman who risked his life to save me," pointing to Rinaldo.

The count answered pettishly, "Your coach stirred up such a confounded dust I had to drop behind." And he smoothed his glossy hair with anxious palms.

The countess said to Rinaldo in her charming voice, "You have not told me your name yet."

"Rinaldo di Paldo, your ladyship, lately captain in the emperor's forces."

"A soldier — think of that, Considine!"

"Very commendable," said the count, trifling with his small chestnut mustache. "Stout fellow, no doubt."

"Don't put on airs, Considine! He is to stay with us at Castle Goldknob, and I shall see that he has every comfort — "

"My angel, is that quite discreet? Have you forgotten that our betrothal ceremony is this evening?"

"Then he shall be the guest of honor. And perhaps," the countess added spitefully, "he may cut a manlier figure than some other people."

"Have it your own way," the count sniffed. "Let one of your footmen ride my horse home. I will sit beside you in the coach, and protect you from further danger."

Rinaldo longed to slap the count's delicate cheek, but just then the countess gave a delighted shriek.

"Considine! Do look what's coming down the road."

It was, of course, the circus on the march. Edward was

overcome by love as usual and broke into a clumsy gallop, and wallowed adoringly at Rinaldo's feet. The other beasts kept ranks, but they all turned their eyes to Rinaldo for orders.

For once Rinaldo wished his beasts were a thousand miles away. But he could not overlook them, so he explained them.

"Ah, splendid, my dear," said Count Considine. "Let them entertain us before the betrothal banquet. It will be most diverting. Five ducats to you, my worthy fellow, if you give satisfaction."

The countess stamped her foot. "Considine, you are impossible. Lord di Paldo is my honored guest. Come, sir, to the castle, you and your beasts; I will lodge them — Considine, you may ride behind."

In this order they approached Castle Goldknob. Rinaldo gave not one thought to his circus performance or to Daffodil. He was in a dream.

Yesterday he had been a prisoner in a dungeon. Now he was the guest of a charming countess, who smiled into his eyes and asked him a thousand flattering questions.

She was a countess in her own right, and the greatest heiress in all these parts. The castle was full of guests for the betrothal; they swarmed into the courtyard to greet her coach.

She gave orders to her steward: "Clear out the north

wing, and give the rooms to Lord di Paldo for his beasts."

Rinaldo protested that his animals were not used to bedrooms, and the steward reminded her that the north wing had been turned over to Count Considine and his suite.

"Do as I tell you!" the countess commanded with flashing eyes, so the pages escorted lambs, bears, dogs and rabbits upstairs to their luxurious quarters.

Rinaldo arranged to show his circus in the courtyard before supper. If the countess was to be betrothed to anyone that evening, he intended she should be betrothed to him.

Count Considine trailed in behind the circus procession, his pretty face gray with dust and red with rage. His squire met him with the news that a mother sheep and two lambs were now established in his bed.

His first impulse was to ride away forever from Castle Goldknob. However, if he did that he would lose the countess's lands and estates, and the upstart Rinaldo would take his place as ruler of these rich domains.

The count was not clever, but his squire was shrewd and wily. Now the squire drew him into a passage, and whispered a plan for taking a quiet part in Rinaldo's entertainment. Count Considine laughed and slapped him on the back, and promised him a thousand ducats if his plan worked.

Rinaldo had had a bath and a fresh suit of clothes. Now he began pacing off the courtyard, planning his entertainment — thirty-eight paces one way, sixty-two the other, all paved with a pattern of round cobblestones. He was humming happily to himself.

The squire watched him, snickering, and then he made a few little arrangements of his own, which he took care Rinaldo should not know about.

The servingmen set torches in iron rings around the walls. The balconies began to fill with guests.

The countess took her place in a gilded armchair, with Count Considine beside her. He ran his hand along under the edge of the railing till his fingers found a loop of cord which the squire had told him to look for. Having found it, he made himself as bewitching as possible to the countess.

The trumpets blew, and down from the north wing came Rinaldo's circus procession, with Wingfoot at the head and the little rabbits bringing up the rear.

Rinaldo carried a long wand. When he came under the balcony he saluted the countess, and she threw him a rose.

Then he put the animals through their marching and countermarching, their games and their dances. Everyone clapped, and the ladies scattered flowers on the cobblestones.

In the entrance arch the poor folk from the village had gathered to watch the show. A young girl whom no one knew made her way into the crowd. She had come a long way, for her bare feet were dusty. Her head and arms were wrapped in a shawl. If people had looked they would have seen, on the hand that held the shawl, a ring with two great pearls. But they were too busy watching the circus.

After the dogs had jumped through their hoops, Rinaldo ordered the beasts to fall back, while he and Wingfoot gave a display of horsemanship.

The knights were able to appreciate the horsemanship, and their cheers rang loudly. The magnificent Wingfoot understood the slightest touch of heel or rein, and went through his paces like a dancer. He leaped over the dogs, then over Edward, next over the sheep and so on, till finally he made a leap over the doe and her fawn, without frightening them.

This was the end of the entertainment. He galloped in a circle, caracoling like a horse in a portrait, while Rinaldo sat easily in the saddle. He was about to salute the Countess de Goldilocks.

No one was watching Count Considine. He gave a sharp jerk to the loop under the edge of the balcony railing.

The loop was the end of a strong, fine-spun cord which the squire had laid across the courtyard and up to the balcony. He had hidden it out of sight, between the chinks of the cobblestones.

Now the count, by jerking the cord, raised it clear of the cobblestones, but in the flicker of torchlight it could not be seen.

It tripped Wingfoot's hind foot, in the middle of one of his curvets. It threw him cornerwise, and he fell all of a heap.

And Rinaldo, who had been gazing up toward the countess — poor Rinaldo flew over Wingfoot's head and landed upside down in a hogshead of rain water, with his boots waving furiously in air.

So neat was this trick that the audience roared with laughter. They thought it was part of the show.

The countess frowned. She did not like to see her new admirer standing on his head in a water butt.

"The fellow is a buffoon," murmured Count Considine. "Amusing certainly, but a buffoon."

The audience was waiting for Rinaldo to come out of the rain barrel. Wingfoot stood drooping, deeply ashamed, for he did not know he had been tripped by a cord.

Rinaldo did not climb out. His boots waved more frantically in the flickering light. The guests began to murmur, "That was an accident. The fellow has no skill — "

The girl in the shawl bounded suddenly across the courtyard. Her shawl fell back and set free a halo of bright gold hair, as blond as the countess's, though not so richly dressed.

"Fools, he is drowning!" cried Daffodil. "Lend a hand." She set her shoulder to the huge barrel to tip it over.

The water spilled out in a torrent, and several pages dragged Rinaldo out of the barrel by the heels. He stood

up choking, dripping and crestfallen. He was almost suffocated, and purple from standing on his head. The crowd screamed with scornful amusement, and Count Considine laughed merrily. He said to the countess, "There's your cavalier who's to sit beside you at the banquet."

"Don't be ridiculous," she said crossly. "He is a fraud. He should be whipped and run out of town."

"Oh, come! The poor fellow has had an accident — throw him a gold piece and send him packing. Look," he went on, leaning gracefully over the railing, "how touchingly that peasant girl is wiping him off with her shawl. She's afraid her hero may catch cold, ha ha!"

The countess tossed her curls. "A charming scene, indeed."

The count intended she should see plenty of Rinaldo in his inglorious state. "Ask them up to the balcony, and give them some money. No doubt he needs it. After all, he saved your life this afternoon."

Rinaldo came unwillingly to the balcony, dripping and shivering, with Daffodil clinging to his elbow. To his dismay, the countess handed him a few gold coins, thanked him coldly, and hoped he had not drunk up all the water in her barrel.

Rinaldo flung the coins over the railing into the courtyard.

In spite of his bedraggled state he looked so handsome and so proud that Count Considine grew uneasy. "Will you present us to your charming wife?" he said with false graciousness.

Rinaldo looked at the Countess de Goldilocks, whom for a little while he had wanted to marry. Her pretty mouth was puckered with scorn. Then he looked down into Daffodil's clear eyes. They were full of sweetness and worship, with a little worry for fear he might have caught a chill. Her feet were bare, but he knew he could trust them to follow him and help him wherever he went.

He took her hand and lifted it. "The lady is not yet my wife, but she does me the honor to wear my ring, and some day I hope she will have me for a husband."

He was suddenly glad he had said this. Daffodil hid her face against the shoulder of his dripping cloak.

"Why, how charming!" cried the countess, relieved that no one need ever know how near she had come to marrying this ridiculous acrobat. "I am celebrating my own betrothal this evening. Let's make it a double ceremony."

The count was delighted with this arrangement. He sent his squire for handsome garments, and ordered two more places set at the high table, and he ran about, telling the guests the news. He did not mean to give the countess a chance to change her mind.

As Daffodil and Rinaldo were crossing the courtyard on their way to the banquet, his foot caught in the cord, which the squire had not had time to take away. "Oho!"

he said. He traced both ends of the cord, and understood why Wingfoot had fallen so awkwardly.

Daffodil cried, "Count Considine is a scoundrel. Will you go in and denounce him?"

"Not at all. I am greatly indebted to him."

"But except for the accident, I do believe the countess would have been willing to marry you."

"Exactly. The count made me look like a fool, and saved me from acting like one."

"But good gracious! Would you rather be married to me than to the Countess de Goldilocks?"

"A hundred times rather."

This answer made them both feel very happy, and they went to the banquet in high good humor.

Next day there was a great double wedding in Goldknob Abbey, and no one could say which bride was the prettier. Rinaldo's animals stood in the abbey porch.

So Rinaldo took Daffodil up on the saddle behind him, and rode away, with his beasts, from Castle Goldknob.

5

Almost by accident, Rinaldo had acquired the best possible wife for him. She went on helping him with the circus, and as they traveled they kept an eye out for a castle to suit them.

This was not easy to find, although as a result of the wars a number of castles were changing hands. They wanted a cosy, medium-sized one with roads and bridges in good order; but such castles belonged to families who had lived in them for three hundred years or more, and who had no intention of moving out. They had given dozens of shows before they found a castle that would do.

It was in bad repair, but they liked its looks. It sat on a crag with handsome mountains behind it, and it had a quantity of little watchtowers with cone-shaped caps. It stood empty, with the gate dangling on one hinge.

They went exploring through echoing cobwebbed chambers, where moth-eaten tapestries still hung. The glass was out of the windows, and rain had dripped through the missing slates of the roof. But in the stable wing Daffodil found a long row of stalls where her beasts could spend the winter. They now had a baby elephant, named Jummo, who caught cold if he felt a draft.

She coaxed Rinaldo, "Surely no one wants this castle as badly as we do."

Rinaldo said, "We must be practical. We must see what land goes with it." But he wanted it too.

In a cottage outside the walls they found an old toothless caretaker. He told them the castle belonged to a nobleman at court, who had inherited it from his uncle killed in the wars. A whole mountain of vineyards and forests went with it, and a prosperous village in the valley.

So Rinaldo took a trip to the emperor's court, to see whether the owner would sell.

He found the owner a thoroughly silly man, willing to sell his castle for half its value so as to get money for a suit of gold armor for tournaments. Rinaldo sold his jewels to the emperor's moneylender, and after paying for the castle he had a good supply of money left over for repairing the roofs and gutters. So Rinaldo rode off for home with the title in his pocket.

The sun made his castle shine out against the purple mountain like a gilded dollhouse. The villagers ran out of their cottages as he came along, bowing and scraping to their new lord, and asking him in the politest way to repair their chimneys, to punish their impudent sons, and to excuse them from paying the last three years' rent.

He and Daffodil hired two servants — old Toothno the caretaker, and a stout widow to cook their meals. For some months they themselves were as busy as beavers putting their property in order.

Rinaldo thought he was the busy one, since all Daffodil had to do was look after a few animals. He was up and down ladders all day, with a foot rule and a mouthful of nails, making repairs.

Looking after a few animals was not as easy as Rinaldo thought. They had the run of the castle. Old Biddy the cook threatened to leave when Jummo's trunk came sliding over her shoulder and helped itself to a cooky. The mice practiced their dancing on the warm hearthstone, and Arthur learned to steer his antlers up the twisting stairway to the parapet, where he liked to walk grandly up and down. Most of the animals produced children that spring, so it was heavy work to feed them and bed them and water them. Daffodil could not go to her own room without some creature following her with a wounded paw to be bandaged, or teasing her to help him jump through a hoop. Her back ached with raising water from the well.

If she had not been so tired the accident would never have happened, because she was a sure-footed country girl. One day she started up from the village, carrying a big sack of butchers' bones for the animals — and she didn't come back to the castle.

By suppertime all the animals were nervous and restless, and Bonzo was moping and moaning like a lost soul. Rinaldo came down from the roof to get her to darn his doublet where he had caught it on a nail, and when he found his wife was gone he was as nervous as his own animals.

Edward Pig had a better nose for following a scent than any dog. Rinaldo took him out into the darkness, and set him to follow Daffodil's trail.

It led them down to the butcher shop in the village, and then part way home again up the mountain; but at a rocky bend in the road it vanished. Edward stood snuffing dismally with his nose over the edge of a cliff.

"Daffodil!" Rinaldo shouted.

Frantic, he called out the villagers with torches, and the animals, and all night they roamed the mountainside. But it was not till daybreak that Bonzo caught sight of Daffodil, lying with her eyes closed, wedged into a cranny between two boulders. He went bucketing down the crags and began licking her face, and Rinaldo was not far behind him.

The villagers came with crowbars and pried the boulders apart, and then made a stretcher to carry her back to Paldo Castle.

She was alive, and after a while she opened her eyes and

smiled at everybody. But her leg was broken in three places.

In those days there was someone in every village who knew how to make splints and poultices, and set broken bones. In this case it was a little old monk from a nearby monastery who had spent his life in doing good. Soon he had her splinted and bandaged and tucked into bed, with a pitcher of herb tea to warm her inside. "But," he said, as he washed his hands before taking his leave, "don't let her try to walk on that leg. I'll come to look at it again in six weeks." And off he hobbled.

At first Rinaldo and the animals were so happy to have Daffodil safe at home that they could not think about anything else.

But breakfast time came once a day, and so did supper-time; and there was no Daffodil to feed them all. The water trough was always empty, and the animals whined for Rinaldo to draw buckets for them from the well — a back-breaking job. Dirty straw piled up in the stables, and there was no one but Rinaldo to shovel it out and lay fresh beds of straw. There were no butchers' bones for the dogs, there was no seed for the birds. Daffodil had attended to all those things.

"I'll be glad when you're up and about again," Rinaldo said to Daffodil one morning.

She gave him a mischievous look, and said, "I'm not sure I shall. It's quite pleasant having my food carried to me for a change."

That look set Rinaldo thinking. He certainly had not meant to overwork Daffodil, but he saw he had. For her sake and his own, he put his mind to inventing some labor-saving devices.

For some days he was busy from sunup to sunset. She heard noises of sawing and hammering in the courtyard and the stables. She heard him training animals: "Hup, there! Hup!" He made speeches to the assembled beasts, which she hoped they understood better than she did.

Finally one morning he came to the bed where she was lying. "I'm going to roll you up in my cloak," he said, "and carry you out on the balcony. It's a beautiful day." That was all he said, but from the sparkle in his eye she knew he had some surprise for her. She could hardly believe what she saw below her in the courtyard.

Rinaldo had built a treadmill which worked an endless chain of buckets from the well to the drinking trough, and he had taught the animals to walk on this treadmill when they wanted a drink. There were Edward and Chico and Bonzo marching along to nowhere, and bucket after bucket of water tilting into the stone trough.

Jummo came walking through the archway, dragging a cart of bones and grain sacks which he had hauled up from the village.

Just then old Toothno opened the stable door. Out came flying a perfect tornado of straw, driven by the brooms in the hands of the two monkeys. The monkeys enjoyed their job so much that after they had finished the stables they leaped and ran along the window ledges of the courtyard, sweeping down last year's birds' nests.

"Why, Rinaldo!" Daffodil cried, her eyes dancing.

"This isn't the half of it," Rinaldo boasted, glowing with an inventor's pride. "Wait till you see the stables. I've built hay chutes. When the big animals want hay, all they have to do is pull a cord with their teeth, and down comes the hay into the manger."

"I can hardly wait. When is Brother Anselm coming to take off this wretched old bandage?"

"Day after tomorrow," said Rinaldo, who had been keeping track with notches on a board.

Daffodil tipped her head so that it leaned against Rinaldo's ribs as he stood beside her. She said dreamily, "I have always loved those animals, but I'm going to love them a hundred times better now that they know how to take care of themselves."

"You're going to have a quiet, easy life from now on," Rinaldo said, "and so am I."

It was several months before he knew how mistaken he was.

6

One fine September afternoon Daffodil and Rinaldo were taking the fresh air on the battlements of Paldo Castle. They could see the peasants harvesting grapes on the slopes of the valley. The animals, fat and sleek, were taking cat-naps in the courtyard.

Daffodil said, "Rinaldo, you are getting fat, too."

"From your good housekeeping, my dear."

"You can't turn handsprings any more, and Wingfoot couldn't carry you over a six-foot gate."

Rinaldo said comfortably, "I've fought for the emperor, and earned a little peace. I mean to grow as fat as I choose; and when I'm too fat to get into my armor, we'll hammer it into soup kettles for the beasts."

"I liked you very well when you were thin," she said, putting her arm through his, "but I'm happy to have you to myself at home. — Why, Rinaldo, who's that riding up the hill — a courier?"

Whoever it was, he drooped in the saddle while the horse painfully climbed the slope. The horse stumbled to its knees and could not rise. The rider dismounted, and led the poor beast, but he staggered, and supported himself by his saddlebow.

"Oh, dear, more trouble," Daffodil said, for all her life she had seen war and trouble.

Rinaldo ran down to lead the man into the hall and give him a cup of wine. "Now," he asked, "what bad news do you bring?"

"Here's a letter," the man said, "from Colonel Gorchy, and thankful I am to get rid of it. If Grumius had caught me carrying it, he'd have cut off my ears."

"Is Colonel Gorchy in danger?" Rinaldo cried.

"Danger! His castle is sacked, and his children are all dead but one, and he himself is held for ransom in the dungeons of Castle Grumius."

The letter was a hasty line, darkened by the smoke of the burning castle where it had been written:

Rinaldo —

Grumius holds me captive for ransom. If my daughter Tamara is still alive, she is unprotected. I have grave wounds. Ask the emperor to send fifty thousand ducats ransom.

Your friend and Colonel,
A. Gorchy

"Who is this Grumius?" Rinaldo demanded.

The messenger's face darkened, and he crossed himself. "A robber, a murderer, a burner of villages. While Gorchy was away at the wars Grumius gathered a band of rascals about him at his castle in the Eastern Marches, and terrorized the countryside. When Gorchy came home he led an attack on Grumius; so Grumius holds him in special hatred."

Rinaldo had food set before Jeremy, the messenger. The poor fellow's hand trembled as he broke his bread. It was plain that he lived in terror of Grumius. With a heavy heart, Rinaldo asked him about Castle Grumius, and he scowled at what he heard.

Daffodil came into the hall, and asked what was the matter. Rinaldo told her, and showed her the letter.

Daffodil knew the story of how Gorchy had saved Rinaldo's life. She said, "You must write the emperor to send the ransom."

"The court is a witless place," Rinaldo said. "If I write, the emperor may not even see my letter." And he paced up and down the hall.

She said timidly, "Perhaps we could sell this castle for fifty thousand ducats."

"Thank you, my dear, for offering to give it up — but who would buy it overnight? Gorchy is dying in his dungeon."

"You owe him your life."

"No question of that," said Rinaldo. "I do not trust the emperor an inch. He lives among his idiotic courtiers. I am sure he spends every penny before it comes in. He will never send fifty thousand ducats in answer to a letter."

"Then you must attend to it yourself," Daffodil said.

"If I were a free man, I would be off on Wingfoot this minute."

Daffodil said quietly, "You are as free as you ever were, Rinaldo, to do your duty."

"Free? I am responsible for one wife, three hundred vassals, and several dozen animals."

Daffodil looked at him with her clear blue eyes. "I've taken charge before," she reminded him. "The sooner you start for the emperor's court the better."

"You're willing to have me go?" he shouted.

"What else can you do?"

"Daffodil, Daffodil, how could you read my mind so well?"

"It is what my own mind would tell me," Daffodil said, blushing, "if I were a man. You must go, and you must not come back till you have rescued Colonel Gorchy."

They spent the rest of the day in planning. Rinaldo made out lists for Daffodil — the names of the villagers, with stars to mark the good ones and crosses for the bad ones; the money that had to go in and out each month; and a map showing the spot on the mountainside where he had buried his last bag of gold pieces.

"Take the gold," Daffodil said. "You'll need it."

"The money Gorchy needs must come from the emperor," Rinaldo said. "Grumius would laugh at my little sack of ducats. I'll take a few in my pocket to get me to court, and be on my way."

Jeremy had been warming himself at the hearth. "Your honor," he said. "May I stay here to look after your lady?"

He did not look like much of a protector, and Rinaldo tried not to laugh. But Daffodil said kindly, "He would be a great comfort to me, Rinaldo."

"I'd like to be in your service," Jeremy said. "You are a true-hearted knight; and let me tell you I have never seen a lady like your wife."

So that was agreed.

Jeremy told them all he knew about Grumius and his band, and drew a map of the road to Castle Grumius. It was a journey of weeks. Daffodil and Jeremy rode a day's journey with Rinaldo when he set off.

"I may be back inside of a week," Rinaldo said as cheerfully as he could. "The emperor will send the ransom."

Daffodil pretended to believe him. She knew it might be months or years before she would see him again.

But they waved and kissed their hands to each other, and said they would meet before long.

7

The journey to court was not long, since the emperor was living in the city of Aix. He had gone there to be crowned, after winning the war; and Rinaldo found the city as busy as an anthill with counts, ambassadors, margraves, and even a few visiting kings and queens. Not only was the palace full, the inns were filled to bursting, and more than one prince was quartered over a butcher shop.

No one stared at Rinaldo and Wingfoot as they picked their way through the crowds to the palace gate. People had finer sights to stare at. He had no dapper squire to follow him. His old trusty armor was shabby and rusted. He felt that the cut of his hair looked countrified — as well it might, since old Toothno had barbered it. But for all that, he looked handsome and soldierly.

It was lucky Wingfoot had been trained to stand alone, since no page offered to hold his bridle. Rinaldo strode into the palace guardroom, and said he had business with the emperor.

This announcement brought catcalls from the guards

AUBERGE
D'AIX

lounging nearby. Rinaldo taught them better manners by knocking a couple of their heads together.

The captain of the guards asked the nature of his business. He said he came on behalf of Colonel Gorchy, who was held captive for ransom.

"Ah, well," the captain said, "tomorrow or next day you can see the chancellor's undersecretary, and if the chancellor approves your affair, he will bring it before His Majesty in a week or two."

"But Gorchy is wounded and in prison. His life is at stake."

"Very likely," said the captain, cleaning his nails. "But the emperor can't attend to your friend till the coronation is over. And I'll be surprised if he has three copper pennies left to rub together after that. He's being put to great expense, to entertain his high and mighty visitors."

Rinaldo said firmly, "Let me at least make an appointment with his secretary."

"You'll have to wait here, and catch him as he goes through. He is dressed in green and yellow stripes, rather like a frog, and his name is Gilbert le Filbert."

While Rinaldo was keeping an eye out for Filbert, a prince and his suite arrived for a visit of ceremony, their garments stiff with fur, brocades and jewels. The emperor's young daughter came in from a picnic, surrounded by gallants and laughing young women; the guards stood to attention as they passed through.

"There goes your Filbert," the captain said, as two green-striped legs scampered up the stairs.

Rinaldo settled himself to wait till Green-legs came back.

A beautiful young knight came through the doorway, with the sunlight glinting behind him. He had armor chased and inlaid with gold, and a sky-blue cloak. His head was wreathed with fresh flowers. He had a gay young face and a flashing smile.

"Who may this ornament be?" Rinaldo growled.

"Why, Count Nimpimm. He's competing in the tournament tomorrow, and he's come to show the princess his new armor. She made him that wreath of flowers with her own hand."

"He looks as if he'd been poured out of barley sugar."

"He's more of a man than he looks, but the Spanish Knight will topple him off his horse tomorrow."

The captain went on to tell Rinaldo about the champion, the Knight of Spain. "No one knows his name, he never shows his face. We'll get our first look at him when he takes off his helmet to accept the prize."

"What makes you so sure he'll get the prize?"

"Oh, there's no doubt about it. He has never been defeated."

"Humph!" said Rinaldo. As a boy he had often ridden in the lists. If he had no serious business afoot, he would have liked to break a spear against this Knight of Spain.

"Here skips your manikin," the captain said.

Rinaldo put himself in Filbert's path. "Sir, may I ask — "

"Later, good friend, I'm at my wit's end with business." Filbert had a long paper in one hand, and a pin in the other.

Rinaldo held his elbow with a muscular grasp. "So am I. I must see the emperor on a matter of life and death."

"What may the matter be?" Filbert asked, while using his pin to make pricks opposite the names on his list.

"The ransom of the famous Colonel Gor — "

The young man stamped his foot and burst into a tantrum. "Ransom! Today of all days, to come bothering me about a ransom. Man, I'm arranging a tournament!"

Rinaldo shook him rudely.

"Oh!" Filbert cried, his frog-eyes bulging. "Let me go, you horrid fellow. Guards, guards!"

"The emperor will crop your ears when he learns that you let Gorchy die."

"Idiot! This is a coronation. Why, even I, Gilbert le Filbert, haven't had a word with His Majesty this past week. Your captive will be dealt with in due time. Enjoy the spectacle today, my angry friend — for it's all you can do."

Rinaldo flung poor Filbert against the wall, and stalked out of the palace. However, he found the little man was right. Today he might as well go down among the tournament tents with the rest of the world.

The tents looked like a field of colored parasols — crimson, yellow, or candy-striped, with flags snapping in the breeze. The curtains were lifted, so that the crowd could stare at camp beds, dinner tables and bustling attendants.

Armorers were clanging away at their forges, pages were oiling the joints in the armor. Grooms were buffing the hoofs of the broad-backed horses, braiding ribbons in their tails, and furbishing the splendid petticoats they were to wear under their saddles. The blacksmiths' hammers rang ding-a-ling against the anvils.

Wingfoot pranced along, supposing he and Rinaldo were part of the show.

Rinaldo felt neglected. In his youth it was his tent the crowd would have gaped at, and his chances they would have bet money on. Now he had as fine a horse as any knight, but nothing else — no squire and pages, no armorer, no elegant pavilion. He envied the Knight of Spain the fun of toppling these curly-headed boys off their horses.

"I will go stare at this Knight of Spain, with the rest of the oafs," he told himself scornfully.

In the whole field of tents like colored morning glories, the Knight of Spain had the only black one. It was as black as ink, and over it flew the scarlet and yellow flag of Spain.

The curtains were pegged close, and guarded by two pages dressed in black velvet, standing with folded arms. Behind the tent a magnificent black war horse stood tethered to a stake. But there was no sign of the Knight of Spain.

"Pooh!" Rinaldo said. "Actors' tricks, to scare the young knights out of their wits."

On a pole in front of the tent hung two shields — the shield of peace and the shield of war. If a contestant rode up and touched the shield of peace with his lance, that meant he wanted to ride one course and break one spear with the knight. If he touched the shield of war, he wanted to fight it out on foot or on horseback with the knight, till one or the other cried quits.

Rinaldo had to admit that the knight was a brave man to fight on such terms. He hankered to get a look at the fellow. After the crowd had gone home to supper he lingered around the sealed black tent.

"The Knight of Spain must eat some time," Rinaldo thought, "and I'll get a look at him then."

A page in black velvet came along the line of tents, but he was not carrying supper. He was slipping secretively along, with another man following him. This other man wore a rusty cape with a pointed hood, his legs were long and spidery, a wisp of beard jutted out in front of his chin, and he carried a satchel.

"There goes a surgeon," Rinaldo said. "Has the Knight of Spain fallen sick?"

The spidery man slid through a crevice in the black tent. Soon Rinaldo heard Spanish cursing, and German jabbering which rose to a squeal.

The tent flap burst open and out bounced Spider-legs,

quivering with rage. The pages followed, begging for his help. However, they spoke no German and he spoke no Spanish. He flung his cloak across his chest and stamped away, while the boys stood wringing their hands.

"Can I interpret for you?" Rinaldo asked them — for during the wars he had picked up several languages.

They ran joyfully after the surgeon and fetched him back.

The surgeon poured out his troubles. "Here is this great Knight of Spain, saying his enemies have poisoned him. He uses very bad language about our emperor."

"He's ill, then?"

"Through his own foolishness. He is so covered with itching hives that he can't put on his armor — but that's because he ate a whole bucket of shellfish last night. He sees two knights and two horses where everybody else sees one — but that's because he drank too much of the emperor's good wine. He's all doubled up with stomach-ache — because he ate a quarter of a wild boar for breakfast."

"What can you do to get him back on his feet?"

Spider-legs hopped up and down with rage. "So! You want me to stand him up on his feet, when he's so stuffed with food and drink that he can only go on all fours like a hog. Are you a Spaniard? Do you think I poisoned him?"

"I am the emperor's man. But if you will tell me the treatment to cure him, I'll explain it to him in Spanish."

"Very well. Tell him to put a hot brick on his stomach, and to eat nothing tonight but a little broth, with this powder dissolved in it."

"Suppose he says the powder is poisoned?"

"Sir, this medicine is compounded from standard drugs: namely, cobwebs from a sooty chimney, crocodile's tears direct from the River Nile, hairs from the tail of a coal-black mouse, and — most precious of all — a shred of His Majesty's last year's jerkin."

"Dear me," Rinaldo said respectfully, and taking the packet in hand he walked boldly into the black tent.

The knight was a fine great ox of a man. In the dim light Rinaldo could see red swellings on his face and hands, and a wet towel tied about his head. He was writhing on his untidy bed, grumbling about assassins and poisoners, and gnawing at a bone of roast meat. Beside him stood a half-empty pitcher of beer.

"Sir, the surgeon wants you take only broth tonight, and this powder."

The knight let fly a cloud of Spanish oaths. "You too!" he cried, struggling to sit up. "You want to starve me, to weaken my strength before the tournament." Rinaldo made allowances for his rudeness, since he was so miserable. When he was not scratching his hives he was hugging his stomach-ache.

Rinaldo shrugged and prepared to take his leave.

Just then, however, the Spanish ambassador came to inquire for the champion's health.

The knight said he would be well by morning, and urged the ambassador not to let the news of his illness leak out around the court. So the ambassador went pompously away.

The knight then opened the packet and sampled the powder. It tasted so horrible that he washed it down with the half-pitcher of beer, and then lay waiting for his health to improve. For some reason it did not do so.

Rinaldo said, "By tomorrow morning if you are too sick to fight, some healthy man can replace you."

"No one can replace me," the Knight of Spain said.

Rinaldo snorted, "I could unhorse you myself."

"Then do my fighting for me, for I — Ow, ow! What a cramp! — I shall not be in tournament trim tomorrow. Ow, ow! That cursed surgeon has poisoned me."

The pages came running with hot broth, hot bricks and hot blankets. "What shall we do?" they asked dismally of Rinaldo.

He answered calmly, "If your master is still sick tomorrow send for me. I will wear his armor and fight his challengers."

"You!" the pages cried scornfully.

But the knight called out, "He will do as well as I shall, at any rate. The chances are I shall be dead and buried by morning. Ow, ow, ow!"

The pages helped Rinaldo try on the knight's glittering black armor. It fitted well enough except around the middle, where they had to stuff it out with pillows. With the visor closed, no one could tell that Rinaldo was not the Knight of Spain.

The pages asked, "Will it please your honor to exercise his lordship's horse? He is a bad-tempered brute, and you will not want to ride him for the first time tomorrow."

Rinaldo halted suddenly. He had been intending to ride Wingfoot. But Wingfoot was gleaming white, and everyone would know he was not the Spaniard's horse.

Rinaldo had not been a circus manager for nothing. He said, "I'll ride my own white horse, but run to the surgeon and ask him for a large brush and a bucket of black, indelible ink."

They brought Wingfoot inside the tent and closed the flaps, and the boys held torches while Rinaldo painted Wingfoot black from nose to tail. Then they hid the real Spanish horse in the bushes, and tied Wingfoot out behind the tent. Rinaldo lay down on the tent floor and went to sleep, while waiting to see whether the Spanish Knight could fight in the morning.

The knight kept on eating and drinking most of the night, and in the morning he was not even slightly better, in spite of the famous powder he had taken. So Rinaldo was to ride in the tournament.

The pages brought hot water for Rinaldo's bath, and

served him a hearty breakfast. He did some gymnastic exercises to limber himself, and the knight swore he had never seen such an athlete.

A squire armed Rinaldo, and an armorer riveted the closings. When he was dressed he obliged the spectators by sitting in the saddle in front of the tent, lance in hand, to be admired.

He and Wingfoot were as black as two cats. His helmet had a gold eagle on the peak. Wingfoot's trappings were of polished black steel and leather, with a sweeping black and gold saddlecloth. His hoofs looked like polished ebony.

The flowery young knights were making their way to the lists where the tournament was to be fought. As they rode up to the Spanish tent and struck their lances against the shield of peace, Rinaldo studied their horses, their weapons and their style of riding.

No one had yet struck the shield of war, and Rinaldo was half glad, half sorry, that he was not to fight any of these young dandies to the bitter end.

Then a knight rode up on a dapple-gray horse, followed by squires and pages dressed in sky-blue and gold. The knight had flowers around his helmet and a lady's scarf flying from his arm. "Count Nimpimm!" the crowd shouted. " — And wearing the princess's own colors."

Inside his helmet Rinaldo gave a scornful smile. But Count Nimpimm laughed, and struck a ringing blow on the shield of war. So Rinaldo had to change his opinion of the elegant young lad.

It was time to go to the lists. The Spanish squire and pages rode before Rinaldo and Wingfoot.

The lists, or runways with fences between, had been set up in a fine level meadow beside the river. At each end were tents for the knights. Along one side was an ornate grandstand for the court dignitaries, on the other a barrier behind which the townspeople could stand.

The heralds blew long blasts on their trumpets, and the crowd cheered the entrance of the emperor and his train, which included his young daughter, the princess.

Then the chief herald read the rules for the tournament and the names of the contestants. Twelve young knights had challenged the Knight of Spain. These twelve were to be paired in six contests; and then the six victors were to take their turn, ending with Count Nimpimm, in riding against the Knight of Spain.

The marshal led a parade of knights around the field. Count Nimpimm made his bow to the princess, who wore his colors of sky-blue and gold, but Rinaldo rode proudly like a Spaniard, and made his bow only to the emperor. The crowd half shivered as he paced along on his superb coal-black charger.

The trumpets tingled through the air, and the first two knights rode out into the lists — Red Feather and Green Feather. Each braced the butt of his lance against his pommel, and guided it with a steel-gloved hand. The crowd cheered for its favorites — Red Feather! — Green Feather!

The trumpets screamed a signal. The two knights struck spurs, and went thundering toward each other.

Clang! Green Feather caught Red Feather square on the breastplate. Both horses staggered, and Red Feather went clattering head over heels into the dust. His pages ran to pick him up, for a man in armor could hardly move except on horseback, and the winner rode proudly to his tent to wait for his turn against the Spanish Knight.

The trumpets sounded again, and the next two contestants rushed together. Rinaldo sat quietly in his tent.

The sun rose hot and high, but no one thought of food or rest. Everyone wanted to watch the Knight of Spain.

As the young knights were eliminated, they went to sit in the stands beside their ladies, till finally only the six winners were left on the field.

By this time Rinaldo had more respect for the six young men who had challenged him. Dandified as they looked, they were well mounted and well trained. And he had five of them to beat before he went into a life-and-death contest with Count Nimpimm.

The pages led out Wingfoot, and Rinaldo rode into the lists. A roar of almost angry excitement greeted him. The crowd wanted Count Nimpimm to defeat him, for the honor of the emperor.

Green Feather sat waiting, spruce and slender, while his

pages tightened his buckles. He looked entirely too cool and self-satisfied to please Rinaldo. "Let's frighten him a little," Rinaldo thought, and touched Wingfoot gently with his spur.

Wingfoot understood that signal from his circus days. He began rearing and pretending to throw Rinaldo off. He rolled his eyes, bared his teeth, danced on his hind legs and struck out into the air with his front hoofs, while Rinaldo sat calm in the saddle.

"He's a demon horse," the crowd muttered, "with a demon rider." The Spanish pages, in terror, tried to drag him down by the bridle, and he swung them clear of the ground.

"Let him be," Rinaldo gave orders through his helmet. "I can handle him." He brought Wingfoot back to earth, and they took their place at the end of the lists. Green Feather was not riding so cockily by now.

Clang! Wingfoot leaped ahead. Rinaldo held his acrobat's body in balance, to dodge Green Feather's lance and to plant his own on Green Feather's breastplate.

They met spear to spear, and Green Feather held his seat in the saddle, but both lances splintered. As they made their way back to the starting point Rinaldo felt Wingfoot still shuddering from the impact. "Give me a new lance," he said.

The next time he rode not so fast, but more craftily. Just before the meeting he gave Wingfoot a sidewise swing. His lance made contact. Green Feather's slid harmlessly past Rinaldo's shoulder, and Green Feather tumbled to the ground.

The Spanish Knight was proclaimed winner of the first bout.

Rinaldo kept his conqueror's bearing, but inside his helmet he began to call himself names. He had been a fool to risk his life for the amusement of a bloodthirsty crowd. If Count Nimpimm defeated and killed him, what would be-become of Daffodil and the beasts? Or of Colonel Gorchy in the dungeons of Grumius? Or of the colonel's young daughter Tamara, who had escaped from the sack of the castle? For their sake, he must fight with all the skill he had, and even so, that might not be enough.

Using all his own veteran skill and that of his wonderful Wingfoot, he knocked over the first four young knights. The fourth was badly lamed in his tumble, and old Spider-legs went scuttling into his tent.

Rinaldo and Wingfoot were glad to rest a minute, for they were tired and winded. But the crowd did not know the champion was tired. The whisper ran like a moaning wind: "The devil himself has come to the city of Aix."

The delay lengthened out. Spider-legs was called to another tent, and soon he came out with a message.

Shortly the heralds proclaimed the surprising news that the fifth knight, Sir Hugo of the White Tower, would forfeit his turn with the Knight of Spain.

The fact was that poor Sir Hugo was so frightened when he saw the fourth knight injured that he fainted dead away in his own saddle, and no powders would put the strength back into his knees. He could not even stand, far less ride his horse. He was obliged to lie down till he got over his fright, so Rinaldo luckily won the fifth round by default.

But now appeared Count Nimpimm, and he was not to be scared even by the devil on a black horse. He meant to fight to the death. Before he closed his visor he blew a kiss to the young princess, and the crowd gave him the biggest cheer of the day.

"Now we're in for it," Rinaldo told Wingfoot. He tested his girth; the squire loosened his dagger in the sheath and called on San Diego for help.

The trumpets blew, hoarse and thrilling. Wingfoot launched straight toward the count's gray war horse.

On the first run they slipped past each other, and the crowd let out its breath in one long sigh. The riders wheeled, and charged again.

This time there was no dodging. Each struck the other square on the visor. Both knights heeled over and crashed out of their saddles, with the horses shivering beside them.

They staggered to their feet in their heavy armor, drew their swords in their right hands and their daggers in their left, and circled each other, watching for a chance to place a blow.

The strokes rang and the sparks flew; the fight swung

evenly back and forth. Rinaldo caught a glimpse of the princess waving her scarf over the balustrade, with anguish in her face. He thought, "If I don't kill Nimpimm he will kill me, and either way, it is a pity."

He should not have taken time for pretty thoughts. He felt a tingling blow on his wrist, and his sword spun out of his hand. His only weapon now was his dagger.

Quick as lightning he came inside Nimpimm's guard, so that the count could not swing his sword, and with his dagger he drove for the chink in the count's armor at the throat. Nimpimm pressed his own dagger against Rinaldo's mailed body.

"Ya-ah!" came the snarling roar of the crowd. Rinaldo had driven home the dagger, and the red blood spurted.

The princess shrieked and covered her eyes. Nimpimm toppled to the ground, and Rinaldo knelt above him.

Now he had a right to make an end of his enemy — but he did not want to. Count Nimpimm was a gallant knight. "Do you yield?" he demanded.

"I yield."

Rinaldo rose to his feet and beckoned Nimpimm's pages. "May we both live," Rinaldo said courteously, "to fight for the emperor in a better cause than this." And he helped lift the groaning young knight to a litter, while the surgeon ran to check the flow of blood. The wound had not gone deep.

Then he walked to the foot of the emperor's dais and saluted him. The heralds announced that the Knight of

Spain had defeated all the challengers and won the tournament.

The emperor said, "Will it please you to lift your visor, and receive the wreath of victory from my daughter's hand?"

Rinaldo raised his visor and let his honest soldier's face be seen. The princess gave him his wreath in a great hurry, so that she could be off to Count Nimpimm's tent.

"Well," said the emperor, "sit down and drink a cup of wine. I envy the King of Spain his champion."

Rinaldo was dead tired, but by fighting his way through the tournament he had earned an interview with the emperor. He mounted the steps and fell on one knee.

"The victory does not go to Spain," he said. "I am one of your own knights. I took the place of the Spanish Knight when he fell ill, because it was the easiest way of getting to speak to you about the business that brings me to court."

The courtiers cried, "Then the emperor has won the tournament after all!" And as the story spread in circles through the crowd, great waves of cheering followed, for no one had wanted to be beaten by a knight of Spain.

Rinaldo was discreet in telling about the sad illness of the Spanish Knight, but he made them all laugh by telling how he had painted his white horse black. The emperor laughed till he nearly rolled off his throne.

"I'll let the King of Spain hear about this," he chuckled. "Next time he sends me a champion, I'll ask for a written description to make sure we have the right man. Well now, Sir Champion, what's this urgent business of yours?"

"Your Majesty remembers the heroic Colonel Gorchy?"

"Vaguely, vaguely," the emperor said.

This vagueness annoyed Rinaldo. He said, "It was the colonel's capture of Plotzen that won the war for Your Majesty."

"True," said the emperor.

"He is held prisoner in Castle Grumius — " And Rinaldo went on to tell about the bandits on the eastern border.

"This must be attended to at once. Rinaldo, I appoint you to go and rescue Colonel Gorchy."

"Sire," Rinaldo answered firmly, "if I had had the necessary supplies I should have been on my way before now. But I need either fifty thousand ducats, or a regiment of troops. That is why I came to court, and played the fool in the tournament."

At this the emperor hemmed and hawed. "Troops! But my troops are disbanded since the Peace, and to get them back I would have to pay them what I owe them, and what would I pay them with?"

"Why, money," Rinaldo said, "out of the taxes."

"But the war was an expensive luxury, my friend — and as for this coronation — Oh, my lord Chancellor, how many ducats had we left in the treasury this morning?"

"Three thousand, Your Majesty," the chancellor replied sourly. "And bills beyond all reckoning."

"So you see, Rinaldo, I am no better off than you are," the emperor said, as if that disposed of the whole matter.

Rinaldo was bitterly angry. On every side he saw pavilions, feasts and jewels. There was money for these, but not for a hero's ransom. But he did not show his anger.

"Very well," he said. "Let me have the three thousand ducats, and I will make them go as far as I can."

The chancellor fairly shrieked, "Your Majesty will surely not turn over the last of your gold to this adventurer!"

Rinaldo was so angry by now that he said, without meaning it, "I have a good mind to go and take service under the King of Spain. He may show more gratitude to his subjects than Your Majesty does."

The emperor really admired Rinaldo, and he knew he himself was not behaving well. "After all," he argued with the chancellor, "what good are three thousand ducats to us? We're going to have to borrow half a million from the skinflint old Duke of Hesse-Boneyard. Let's give Rinaldo the three thousand to come and go on."

He invited Rinaldo to the banquet at the palace, but Rinaldo said he wanted to set off that very afternoon.

"You're not going alone, surely — "

"Since Your Majesty has no one to send with me." But his one-man adventure against Grumius did sound desperate, even to him.

He bathed in the Knight of Spain's tent, and dressed in his own old battered armor. The pages scrubbed the ink off

Wingfoot as well as they could, but he still looked streaky.

He was packing up the bag of ducats when he noticed three figures standing in the door of the tent. "What can I do for you?" he asked them.

Three young men came shyly inside, and introduced themselves by the names of Tom, Dick and Harry. They were squires from the tournament, but when they had heard about Rinaldo's knightly adventure of rescue they had lost interest in curling the courtiers' hair and braiding the horses' manes. They wanted to follow Rinaldo to the Castle of Grumius.

"I can't pay you," Rinaldo warned them.

They did not want to be paid. They came from noble families, and each had his own horse and weapons.

"Then God bless you, and I make you welcome," Rinaldo cried. He had been heartsick at the selfishness of the court, and these boys restored his faith in knighthood.

So when he rode eastward out of Aix, he was followed by three strapping young lads on fine horses.

8

For three days they rode gaily, with Tom, Dick and Harry whistling and joking. Rinaldo taught them how to camp in the forest, and they slept wrapped in their cloaks beside the fire.

On the fourth day they came to a wide river where the bridge was gone. The water swirled fiercely around the broken piers.

Tom asked an old fellow whether there was a ferry.

"Ah, you must call Broomstraw Hilda," he said. "There she sits with her back turned, on the point yonder, watching you in her mirror."

"Just call her, will you? Here's a penny for you."

"Not I," the old man said with a shudder. "To make her come you must stand in the exact center of this white stone, on your left foot, and turn around three times without touching your right foot to the ground. That will bring her, and nothing else will."

"She sounds like a queer customer."

"A very queer customer!" And the old man made a sign to keep off the evil eye.

Rinaldo thought this was a nonsensical way to call a ferrywoman; but after they had hallooed till they were tired, he tried the old man's method. No sooner had he turned around three times than the tattered old creature got to her feet and came toward them along the riverbank, walking backward and watching them in the mirror she held in front of her face. She was towing a huge washtub beside her in the water. Her tattered petticoats were a mass of pockets, out of which dangled beads and dishes. She wore gold rings on her bare brown toes. Fastened to her belt on one side was an old broom of twigs, which trailed in the dust; on the other side, the chain for her mirror. It was many a day since she had combed her hair. She wore earrings that swung against her withered neck, and she had only three teeth. "At your service, my pretty lads," she cackled.

Rinaldo said, "Why didn't you come when we called?"

"Ah, I must see you in my mirror first — that's the rule." She drew her tub up to the bank and plumped herself down in it, using her broom for an oar. She held out her hand invitingly. "One at a time. You first, young man!"

The tub was bobbing in the current. Harry held back, and said, "I mistrust this old beldam."

Rinaldo said, "I'll make the first trip, and Wingfoot shall

swim behind." And bridle in hand, he stepped into the tub.

"Have you a ducat for the fare?" Hilda croaked.

Rinaldo said shortly, "I'm on the emperor's business."

She gave him a glittering look and put out into the stream. In her hands the broom made a surprisingly good oar. When the current carried them toward rocks and whirlpools it swept them back out of danger. Wingfoot swam behind with his great head plowing the surface, and his body serving as a rudder. Soon they were halfway across. But suddenly she stopped paddling.

"What are you doing?" Rinaldo shouted — for the tub was drifting toward the broken arches of the bridge.

She sniffed with her old parrot nose. "I can't be mistaken," she said. "That's gold I smell on you."

"You smell one ducat, neither more nor less, and you don't get that till you earn it."

"I smell thousands of ducats, thousands. If you want to land safe on the far shore, let me have them. If not — " She showed her horrid teeth.

"Robbery! So that's it." The tub lurched as Rinaldo leaped for the old woman's throat. "Ply your broom, before I squeeze the breath out of your body."

"Give me your gold," she said coolly.

They were bearing down on a stone pillar, where they must upset, and loaded as he was with the emperor's ducats, Rinaldo could not swim. He snatched for old Hilda's broom.

"Don't you dare touch that broom," she shrieked. "It is a magic broom, and it takes orders only from me — Broom, drown this rascal!"

"Rubbish," said Rinaldo, and began paddling.

She clambered toward him like a wildcat. To keep her away he swept her face with the bristles.

"Don't," she gasped. "Ha-ha-ha — tee-hee-hee! Oh, don't — I can't stand it — I'm ticklish." And she laughed and cried at the same time, till she was limp.

Rinaldo kept the broom and paddled to the shore, using it to tickle Hilda from time to time to make her behave. Each time she doubled up in a helpless agony of laughter.

When they landed she said meekly, "Give me back my broom, and I will go back and bring your friends over."

Rinaldo said, "I don't trust you. I'll leave you here on the bank, and I'll paddle back for my friends."

He ferried them across one after another — Tom, Dick and Harry, each with his horse swimming behind.

"What are you going to do with the old lady's broom?" Harry asked while they were making the last crossing.

"I'm going to break it over my knee. She has persuaded everybody that it is a magic broom, and she has used it to keep her neighbors in terror."

"How sad she looks," Harry said. Hilda had dropped to the ground like a bundle of rags. She was wiping tears from her eyes, and her hand reached out longingly toward the broom Rinaldo was carrying.

He had not paid his ferry fare. Although he had done the paddling, he had done so with Hilda's tub and Hilda's broom, so he reached into his pocket and threw a ducat over to her.

"I'd rather have my broom," she whimpered.

"It's not a magic broom at all," he told her. "You are not only a bad old woman, you are a silly old woman. You've used it to terrify people and rob them and drown them."

"It's my only friend," she wailed.

He said, "I'll give you back your broom on one condition. Broomstraw Hilda, is there a name by which you will swear, and keep your oath?" He did not ask her to swear by the name of God, since she thought herself a witch, and witches swore by the devil.

"Yes, my lord," she whispered, yearning for her broom.

"Well then, if you will swear to do good with your broom instead of mischief, I'll give it back to you."

He saw the struggle in her face, for she was full of wickedness. Finally she raised her hand, with her fingers twisted into a secret sign, and spoke some words in gibberish.

Silently he handed her the broom. She patted and comforted it as if it had been a lost child. She looked up suddenly.

"But how can I keep myself occupied, now that I have promised not to do wickedness any more?"

"You can go home and use your broom to sweep out your house. I am sure it needs it. After that you can do good among your neighbors, whom you have scared out of their wits for so long."

Broomstraw Hilda sighed; she did not find this prospect exciting. But she had sworn not to do evil, so she climbed into her tub and paddled gloomily home to her cabin on the riverbank.

9

The four adventurers rode eastward in the fine autumn weather. Roads and bridges were being put in order after the war, and old soldiers were tinkering with repairs around their cottages.

But when they came to the Eastern Marches it was another story. There were no cattle in the fields. Houses stood burned and roofless. When the villagers saw four armed men approaching, they ran home and barred their doors.

The peasants talked in a harsh dialect that Tom, Dick and Harry could not understand. But Rinaldo had learned this dialect during his campaigns, and he talked to the innkeepers.

What he heard made him frown darkly. Grumius and his marauders had laid the country waste. There were orphans in every village. Churches had been wrecked and their treasures carried away. He met men who had had their ears cut off because they had resisted Grumius.

"We must wipe out this Grumius once and for all," he growled.

They pointed out the fire-blackened ruins of Gorchy's castle. "That is what he got for standing up to Grumius," they said. "His castle was burned and his family was all killed. The rest of us dare not raise our heads."

"All killed? I understood that the colonel's daughter escaped."

They told him sadly, "She did escape and took refuge with some woodcutters in the mountains, but the raiders followed her and burned the woodcutters' hut, and the poor young lady was found dead in the ashes. She is buried in our village church."

Rinaldo burned with new anger as he visited the tomb. The letters cut on the tomb said:

TAMARA
Only Daughter of Athanasius Gorchy
Foully Done to Death in the
XV Year of Her Age

He asked the road to Castle Grumius. They told him he must go through a winding pass in the mountains, following the course of a river. Where the road was narrowest he would find it blocked by a castle that stood between cliff and stream, and that would be Castle Grumius.

So they made their way into the mountains. Winter was

coming on; the wind blew keen. As they went higher they saw snow drifted in the crevices of the rocks.

The young squires looked grave.

"Do you want to turn back?" Rinaldo asked them. "There are still tournaments at court, and pretty young ladies."

They laughed scornfully. They had come to rescue Colonel Gorchy. "Only," they said, "it's a pity the emperor did not send a larger troop. Four men do not make much of an army."

Rinaldo laughed and said, "When a general is short of soldiers, he has to fall back on his wits."

The road climbed and twisted among the rocks, going higher and higher. A storm wind blew down from the peaks, carrying a blinding snowstorm. Wingfoot went first, picking the way, but even he could not keep the road. The snow whipped their faces like great, blowing curtains. They blundered into drifts. Finally even Wingfoot could go no further.

They spent the night huddled miserably against their horses. Rinaldo set his young men to scrape under the snow for firewood, and then to melt snow in their helmets for drinking.

The snow stopped falling. The rising sun showed them a world lonely, white, empty and beautiful. There was no sign of a house or a road.

"Sir," Dick asked suddenly, "is this mountain a volcano?"

"Certainly not."

"Then why is smoke coming out of the ground?" And sure enough, a corkscrew of smoke was twisting up out of a pit in the snow.

They went floundering off through the drifts to explore. To avoid sinking they had to throw themselves on their faces and wriggle along.

Rinaldo saw them reach the smoke-hole and peer down. Then suddenly they began to scratch and dig furiously with their bare hands.

They gave a shout. They had uncovered the top of a brick chimney. They were standing on the roof of a buried house. They used their hands as a dog uses his paws, throwing out spurts of snow between their legs. Rinaldo joined them at their work.

"Are there people inside?" he asked.

"Yes. We heard a child calling to us."

Soon they had cleared an attic window. A little boy's laughing face appeared, round as an apple. He handed them out a shovel, so that the work went faster.

One side of the roof sloped straight down to the mountainside, and soon they were standing on solid ground. Then they cut a trench around the corner to the front door, laughing and whistling and taking turns with the shovel. Soon the doorway was clear enough to open. They trooped in to enjoy the warmth.

It was a tiny, one-room cabin, with a fire blazing on the hearth. The tables, benches and cupboards were of old carved wood. Dried onions and smoked meat hung from the rafters. The family beds stood behind cupboard doors at the end of the room.

Best of all, a kettle was bubbling over the fire, and sending up a savory steam. But they saw no one except the little boy, and he talked to them in gibberish.

Since there was no one to give them permission they began filling their basins with stew from the pot. But at this the little boy looked shocked, and pointed to one of the bed cupboards.

Dick said jokingly, "Won't your old grandmother spare us a meal, even after we've dug her out of a snowdrift?" And he threw open the bed cupboard.

All he could see was a tumble of featherbeds, and a foot in a woman's shoe. The woman had dug herself under the covers for safety. He began tossing pillows right and left. "Come out, Grandmother," he shouted, "and invite us to dinner."

A slight figure sat up straight, clutching the quilts across its chest. Dark, hunted eyes stared out at them.

Rinaldo said, "Come out, good woman. You have nothing to be afraid of."

She climbed out of bed and stood trembling.

"Is that your idea of a grandmother?" Harry mocked Dick. For this was a girl, a young girl just beyond childhood.

She was pale and half-starved. Her black eyes darted from face to face, and she was ready to jump and run.

Rinaldo spoke to her courteously in several languages, but she gave no sign of understanding him. So he pointed to the stew kettle, and then inquiringly to his mouth.

At that she nodded. She ran to fetch a loaf of bread, and cut slices for them — constantly shrinking back as if she expected a blow.

Soft-hearted Dick coaxed her to sit and eat with them, but she was too frightened. The more they saw of the poor girl the more eager they were to take revenge on Grumius.

Rinaldo said, "These children must be alone in the world. No doubt their parents are dead, and the girl is taking care of her little brother."

The girl and the boy sat down in the corner and finished what the men had left in the pot, but they noticed that she put some of the supper aside in a covered bowl. Next she set a lighted candle in the window. She was expecting someone.

After supper they led their exhausted horses to the shed behind the house and gave them some hay. Tom said, "I have a mind to sleep out here myself, rather than scare the poor young maid out of her wits, by going back into the house."

Dick said, "We must show the poor pretty little thing we don't mean her any harm." He took from around his neck a trinket his sister had given him, which he always wore. It was a tiny gold cross on a chain.

He went back into the hut, and gently held this out to the girl. Her dark liquid eyes looked at the cross, and then at Dick's pleasant face. She stopped trembling.

He stepped forward and put it around her neck, lifting the curly tendrils of her hair. She picked up his hand and kissed it, holding her own hand over the cross as if it were a treasure.

Harry said, "Dick's tamed the wild bird."

Dick said firmly, "Anyone who harms this wild bird will have to settle with me."

At bedtime the girl and the little boy crept inside one bed cupboard so as to leave the other for Rinaldo, but he chose to take his luck with his squires, rolled in his cloak before the fire.

Early next morning they heard halloos outside. The youngsters were wildly excited. Everyone went out, and helped bring in the father of the little household, who was frozen and exhausted from his night in the storm. For twenty-four hours he did nothing but sleep.

Later, however, he and Rinaldo had long talks about Castle Grumius and the best way to attack it. The man shook with rage whenever he heard Grumius's name.

Rinaldo consoled him, "You still have your roof over your head, and your family."

"My home? My family? This is not my home. I took refuge here when Grumius burned my cabin in the forest. And my wife — "

"What happened to your wife?"

"You are a stranger, you would not know. My poor wife was burned to death in trying to save our little Countess Tamara, who had taken shelter with us."

"Tamara!" Rinaldo poured out questions. At first the peasant answered distrustfully. "Pardon me, sir, if I am cautious with you, but the raiders scoured the whole countryside to find the little countess, and tracked her to my hut, and then they set fire to it to drive her out. Oh, the weary year we've had."

Rinaldo assured the man he had come to rescue the colonel and punish Grumius.

"I wish you had come sooner. You might have saved her ladyship. Now all you will see is her tomb."

"I've seen it. I've knelt there and made a vow."

"Ah, so?" said the man, in his half-doubtful tone. "Well, good luck to you. When you come back successful, I will tell you the whole story of my wife's death — but not now. The snows are melting fast, the road is clear, and you had better be on your way."

Rinaldo went to call the squires. Tom was chopping wood, Harry was whittling a toy soldier for the little boy. Rinaldo asked where he could find Dick.

"Try the stable, sir," they said, and laughed.

The stable was dark, and it seemed to be empty. "Dick!" Rinaldo called.

Dick answered from above Rinaldo's head, "Oh, sir, do you need me?"

Rinaldo looked up and saw two pairs of legs dangling from the beam — Dick's long shins, and a girl's petticoats and little black shoes. The two of them were working at something — Dick had a nail and a hammer. "There, I've finished," he said. "Coming, sir!" and down he jumped.

The girl was threading something on the gold chain he

had given her, alongside the cross. It was half of a gold coin that Dick had broken in two. He had hammered a hole through it with his nail.

"What game is this?" Rinaldo asked.

"No game at all, sir. Something entirely serious." Dick looked up at the girl, kissed the half of the coin that he held in his hand, and slipped it into his pocket.

"In what language do you talk to the young maid?" Rinaldo asked.

"Oh," said Dick in high spirits, "we chirp — like two birds."

The adventurers mounted and took the road. The peasants waved them good-by, and the young girl kissed her hand. Dick whistled gaily as he rode.

Rinaldo came alongside on Wingfoot, and said gravely, "Dick, you are in my charge. You should not have given a peasant girl the gold token. She will expect you to marry her."

Dick said, "I expect to marry her. But she is no peasant girl."

Rinaldo cried, "Was it the Countess Tamara, then?"

Dick nodded. "Yes — but don't tell the others. She will be safer if not even her friends know she is alive. People would chatter, and Grumius would be on her trail again."

"She told you all this? In what language?"

"Oh, she talks our language perfectly well. But for safety's sake she pretends to be an ignorant peasant."

Dick told Rinaldo that when the woodcutter found his wife's body in the ashes he decided to bury it as if it were Tamara's, to save the girl from being hunted further. In the grave marked with the name of the peasant's wife nothing was buried except a log rolled in cloth. No one knew the secret except the old priest who had made the arrangements.

For Tamara had run away into the forest when the raiders came.

10

Rinaldo and the squires rode secretly into Grumius's country. Each time they climbed a ridge they scouted for danger before they went down into the next valley.

On the second day they saw a black column of smoke rising. This meant that the raiders were burning and plundering a village. People were being robbed and perhaps murdered.

Rinaldo left Wingfoot hidden in a thicket, and climbed to a point of rock from which he could see the whole valley. He set himself to thinking out his plans.

But a plan was not easy to make. He could not ransom Gorchy with only three thousand ducats. And how could he attack a castle with only four men?

He must enter the castle by a trick, and carry Gorchy out of it by luck, wit and courage.

Rinaldo did not want to throw away four lives on an adventure that did not even do Gorchy any good. He needed to know what the inside of the castle was like. But the peasants could not tell him. Those of them who went in did not come out alive.

He must push ahead and make his plans from moment to moment.

Far below him he could see a distant scrap of road between the hills. He could see some moving specks, two, three — a ragged column of little specks.

They were horsemen galloping fast, with loads behind their saddles. They were the plunderers from Castle Grumius, but they were not heading toward home; they were looking for another town to pillage.

There was one horse swifter than the rest; it moved

like a feather on a breeze. This must be an advance scout.

The group came into sight on a nearer loop of the road. Rinaldo counted forty or fifty riders.

The fast-running horse, far in the lead, halted and whinnied. To Rinaldo's horror, Wingfoot whinnied back. The rider instantly turned off across country, toward Wingfoot.

This rider hunched like a monkey on his horse's back, and came straight over rocks and gullies. Rinaldo could not move without being seen on his rock, so he loosened his sword and dagger and prepared to fight.

The rest of the robbers did not turn off the road. The single horse came picking its way up the sharp slope.

Rinaldo stepped out into view, scowling his blackest. But to his astonishment the rider made a friendly signal, and Rinaldo saw he was not armed. He was a little bright-eyed hunchback, with a great bundle behind his saddle.

"Good day, friend," he called from below. "Have you any need for peddlers' wares?"

"Peddlers' wares!"

"If you'll come down," the little man said, grinning, "we can trade more privately."

This might be a trap, but Rinaldo could not stay on his rock forever. He clambered cautiously down.

The little fellow guided him to a ledge out of sight of the road, slid out of the saddle and opened his peddler's pack. "Needles and pins," he chanted, "a penny apiece. Or pewter plates from the village you see burning yonder."

"You rascal! — Peddling the stolen goods even before the fires are out."

The little man shrugged. "Someone must buy from the raiders, or why should they bother to go raiding? I have nothing here of much value," he said scornfully. "This valley was picked bare before I got here. But here's a bit of velvet from a church — your lady might like it."

"My lady does not care for plunder from churches."

"Well, then, here's a packet of spices from Baghdad, honestly bought and paid for."

The peddler had a mischievous eye deep sunk under his brows, and a naughty grin. He went on, "I write letters for my good customers. The brave lads at Castle Grumius are unhandy with a pen."

Rinaldo asked sharply, "Then you've been inside Castle Grumius?"

"Oh, I go and I come. Nobody thinks enough of Jocko to rob him. I go to fine houses. One day before Castle Gorchy was burned, I rode in there and sold back to the colonel the silver dishes the robbers had stolen from him."

"You know Colonel Gorchy?"

"Like my own uncle," Jocko said impudently. "Now that he's in prison he hires me to carry out letters for him." And his eyes twinkled more knowingly than ever.

Rinaldo was tremendously excited. He said, "What's the news of Colonel Gorchy? I knew him in the wars — in prison, you say?"

"Oh, he's ailing, sadly ailing. He won't live long. He lives underground in a damp dungeon, with only enough food to keep him alive till his ransom is paid. He's expecting a friend to come with his ransom, but the friend has not arrived." And Jocko squinted at Rinaldo.

"You have a message for me," Rinaldo cried.

The little man pulled out a letter and peered at it. "Not unless your name is Rinaldo di Paldo," he said.

"Let me have it!"

Jocko dodged like a hare, and leaped into his saddle, where he sat laughing down at Rinaldo. "Fifty ducats is the price of this letter," he said.

"Fifty ducats! I'll give you five."

"Oh, very well," Jocko said saucily. "I must find another buyer. Grumius will give me my price for it." And he set his horse in motion.

He meant to ride away from Rinaldo, who was on foot. But Rinaldo caught Jocko by the leg. He pulled him off his horse and gave him several sharp cuffs. "That will teach you to be saucy to your betters," he said.

"Oh, you're killing me," Jocko squealed. "Mercy, mercy! Here, you may have your letter."

Rinaldo paid him the five ducats, and opened the letter. It asked him to hurry with the ransom, because Gorchy was wounded, and starving in his dungeon.

Rinaldo asked thoughtfully, "How did you know I would be here this morning?"

"Oh, there are tall tales abroad about your honor — very tall tales indeed. I've heard about the Knight of Spain, and about the emperor's three thousand ducats — I've told Grumius that the great Rinaldo di Paldo is on his way with a troop of soldiers and three donkey-loads of gold pieces. I've suggested that the snow has delayed you — that's why he's gone raiding this week, so as to be on hand for you a week from now."

Rinaldo said stiffly, "My troop of soldiers is a day behind me on the road."

"Tut, tut, your honor — such fibs! You have no soldiers. You have only three apple-cheeked lads. I almost fell over one of them in the thicket yonder. He had hidden himself right craftily behind a bush, so that nothing showed except both ends of his great fat horse."

Rinaldo could not help laughing. In a strange way he

liked the queer little creature. He was ashamed to have struck a cripple. He took out another five ducats and tossed them to Jocko.

Jocko stared at the generous knight who had offered him five ducats for a letter, snatched it by force, and then paid him ten. "Many thanks, your honor. I haven't met many men like you and Colonel Gorchy. — Well, I'm heading back for Castle Grumius. If we meet there let's meet as strangers, for safety's sake."

"I suppose there's no use in asking you to help me. You would take my money and learn my plans, and then sell my secrets to Grumius."

The little man kicked at a pebble for several minutes. Then he said slowly, "I have known but two gentlemen of honor — you and Colonel Gorchy. I would rather serve you than that wild boar Grumius."

"If I could trust you I would hire you."

"You have no reason to trust me," Jocko said sadly. "I have been crooked all my life. When I was a small lad my master broke my bones when he had been drinking — that's why my back is twisted. I've never had a friend, except my mare Lelia."

"She's a beauty."

Jocko smoothed her neck, and she whickered in his ear. "She's not one of your great clumping war horses," he boasted. "Her mother came from the sultan's stable in Constantinople."

Rinaldo said, "I have a horse down the hill there that I wouldn't trade for the sultan's own charger." So they went down to look at Wingfoot, and fortunately each of them continued to prefer his own horse. Jocko said, "I've been offered a thousand ducats for Lelia, but she's not for sale. She's my family — my wife and children."

Rinaldo was drawn to the shifty, merry, unhappy little man, and it was plain that Jocko felt the same way toward him.

"Your honor," Jocko proposed suddenly, "if I put Lelia in your hands as a pledge — if I left her with your friends down the valley — would you hire me to help you in and out of Castle Grumius?"

Tears stood in Jocko's deep-set eyes. He was offering his only treasure. Rinaldo said, "I couldn't use your mare — she's too light for me, but on the day I bring Gorchy out of the castle I'll give you a thousand ducats. And while you're in my service I expect you to live like an honest man."

"Oh no, your honor," Jocko protested. "I understand wickedness better than you do. I should be no help to your honor if I lived honestly."

"Well," Rinaldo said laughing, "at least I shall expect you to work honestly for my money."

And this Jocko promised faithfully.

Jocko drew a map of Castle Grumius in the dirt, and marked the entrance to the dungeons.

"You must get in and out before the raiding party comes back," he said, "while there is only a small garrison. I'll do my part by riding with the robbers, and urging them farther and farther away from home, so as to give you time. You can probably count on three days. But as to how you're to get inside the castle, I have no ideas at all. You can't very well pretend to be peddlers — you don't look the part."

"Leave that to me," Rinaldo said. "I have ideas."

Jocko gave him a half-mocking salute from the saddle, and set off on his light-running mare to join the marauders.

II

Rinaldo, with Tom, Dick and Harry, made his way into the heart of the mountains. There were no trees but stunted pines. An eagle screamed above them. Three times they forded the rushing river.

Suddenly, as they came around the corner the road ended at a drawbridge and a great barred gate. This was Castle Grumius.

A sentinel hailed them grimly from the wall above.

"We want to see Grumius," Rinaldo shouted.

The sentinel scratched his chin and disappeared.

Soon the commanding officer appeared. "Friend or foe?" he asked.

"Oh, friend," Rinaldo said with a laugh. "We want to join Grumius's band and share his plunder."

"Then you're not bringing a ransom from the emperor?"

"Emperor?" Rinaldo said bitterly. "Now that the emperor has won the war, he has no money for his old officers. We want to make our fortunes by banditry, as Grumius does. Perhaps *that* will teach the emperor a lesson!"

"Well," said the officer, "that was how I came to join Grumius myself. After all, if you were enemies you would not be such fools as to put your heads into a trap. You may come inside."

The drawbridge swung down, the spiked portcullis rose, and the gates opened. Tom, Dick and Harry rode behind their leader into the courtyard.

It was a narrow castle between cliff and river. The buildings climbed the cliff like swallows' nests, and the courtyard was like the bottom of a well, with the sky for a lid. Crooked steps went up to the keep, with arches under them that led to the stables.

"Stay clear of the dog," the officer said. "He'll nip your horses' heels. He guards the dungeons."

The dog was tied to an iron ring in the wall, beside the door of the dungeon. He was a ferocious great gaunt beast; his eyeballs were bloodshot and his jaws slavered as he tried to reach the newcomers.

They stabled their horses, and the officer led them up to the great hall, where a haunch of venison was turning on the spit. On benches along the wall men were loafing and throwing dice.

Rinaldo put on a jolly, rascally look. This was a hard job, since the castle disgusted him. The whole place smelt of mold and cobwebs. Old meat bones were scattered on the floor, and mangy dogs were mumbling them. The corners were cluttered with loot — saddles and ironware, dishes, armor and furs.

It was the robbers who disgusted him most. They had matted hair and bristling chins, snaggle-teeth and shifty eyes. They swore and snarled over bits of the plunder. They were the riff-raff of half a dozen armies.

But Rinaldo made himself as agreeable as if they were visitors to his circus. He told them stories about the wars, and encouraged them to boast about their villainous adventures. "This is the life for me!" he cried. "How about it, Tom? — Hey, Harry?"

The squires rambled out into the courtyard and chatted with the guards. There were always three on duty, who kept the keys to the gate and the dungeon, and turned them over to the next watch.

"You must have hundreds of prisoners down there," Dick said.

"Not over a dozen. We don't save them alive unless they can command a ransom. Colonel Gorchy, now — he's a pet of the emperor's. We expect to make a fortune out of him."

"So you feed him well, to keep him alive till the ransom arrives?"

The guards looked guiltily at one another. While Grumius was away they had neglected to feed the prisoners, and if one of them starved, the guards would be to blame.

So one of the guards fetched a bucket of gruel and a dipper; and the captain with his keys opened the door that led down to the dungeons.

But when Tom strolled over to look down, the captain called out sharply, "Now, now! — keep your nose out of that."

A cold, dank air blew up the stairs. Water trickled down the walls. Down went the guard with pail, dipper and torch.

Late at night, when the bandits were asleep, Rinaldo and the squires held a conference in whispers. Harry said, "There's no chance of forcing the door, and getting past the dog and the guard. And how could we open the great gate?"

"By strategy," Rinaldo said. "You remember how Broomstraw Hilda kept a whole village terrified with nothing but a tub and a mirror and an old twig broom. We are going to terrify these scalawags."

Tom objected, "If they catch us they will cut us into small bits."

"We mustn't let them catch us. Go to work, boys — fill this castle with ghosts and witches."

Tom settled down for the night beside an old wooden chest. He began operations by reaching out in the darkness and rapping sharply on the underside of the chest.

One of the bandits stirred restlessly, but nobody woke.

Tom rapped again, clappity-clap.

Harry let out a piercing shriek, like a man in a nightmare. "What was that?" he screamed.

The bandits cursed and told him to be quiet. "It was a rat. We have thousands of rats."

In another ten minutes — clappity-clap, louder than before. Harry staggered to his feet. "Let me out of this place!" he shouted. "Look, there's blood dripping out of that chest."

Dick rose noisily to quiet him. "There's no blood," he soothed him, " — or at least, not *much* blood."

The rapping came again — clappity-clap!

"That's no rat," Harry shrieked. "I've heard that noise since I was a child, and it's an omen of death. They say," he went on gruesomely, "it's the ghost of a murdered man, trying to get at his murderers. One night I heard such a rapping, and in the morning my uncle was found dead in the courtyard. Does that chest belong to someone who was murdered?"

"It came from the archduke's hunting lodge," one of the bandits remembered. "It seems to me we cut the watchman's throat." And they looked uneasily at one another.

For the rest of the night they stayed away from that end of the hall, but the squires saw to it that they got no sleep. Rappings came from the doors and hallways, and Harry obliged them with more nightmare shrieks.

With daylight they forgot their fright. Rinaldo entertained them in the courtyard with gymnastic tricks.

While he was turning cartwheels they said, "Do stay clear of that dog. He's ravenous with hunger. He'll take a hunk out of you as you go by."

"I'm fond of dogs," Rinaldo said. "I'll show you how to handle him. — Dick, bring me a marrowbone."

Rinaldo walked toward the dog with the bone in his hand, speaking pleasantly to him. The bandits roared with laughter, expecting that when the dog snatched at the

bone he would take off Rinaldo's fingers in the same bite.

No one had ever spoken pleasantly to the dog before. He was too surprised to growl. Rinaldo held the bone just out of reach, where the dog could sniff it. He whimpered with longing.

"Shake hands politely, sir," Rinaldo said, "and you shall have your dinner."

The dog could not imagine what Rinaldo was talking about, but he wanted that bone desperately. Rinaldo reached out and tapped his forepaw. The dog raised it clumsily, hoping that was what Rinaldo was asking him to do. Rinaldo shook his paw respectfully, and immediately handed him the bone. Then he patted his head.

From that moment the dog was his adoring slave. But the robbers had no idea that he and Rinaldo were now intimate friends.

Jocko came wandering back on foot; he had left Lelia outside the walls. "Who are these strangers?" he asked sharply, pointing to Rinaldo's men.

"New recruits, and good ones."

"I hope you're right," he said, "or Grumius will crop your ears."

He made their eyes pop with reports of the rich plunder Grumius was collecting. It would be another two days before he came back.

That evening was most unpleasant. The trouble began at supper, when a plate came skimming through the air and caught fat Olaf in the ear. Dick screamed, and said an ice-cold hand had come past his shoulder to throw it.

Natobar rushed in, babbling a dreadful story: as he passed through a dark archway an ice-cold hand had tried to hold him back. If he had not been too frightened to look he might have discovered that Dick had just dipped his hand in the ice-cold water bucket.

There were raps on the windowpanes, and hollow groans from the tower. And blood-curdling sounds which Harry made by putting his head inside a large stone jar, and blowing ear-splitting blasts on a hunting horn from inside the jar.

Rinaldo stayed close to the fireside circle, spinning story after story about ghosts and witches — all of whom, if you could believe Rinaldo, spent their time making life a burden to murderers.

When the watch was changed at midnight, the guards came in shaking with fright. They too had been hearing howls and feeling icy hands. (Jocko had strolled out to the battlements, it happened.) The captain had all he could do to make the next watch take its position, and they stayed as close together as they could.

The following night was the last night for Rinaldo's rescue, and he was not happy about it. In a crisis, the bandits might not be as cowardly as they seemed.

However, at supper the captain almost created a mutiny by reading off the names of that night's watch.

"I haven't been feeling well," the first man said.

Another said, "I promised my good mother always to be in bed by nine o'clock."

A third said that the ghosts had made off with one of his shoes, and he couldn't be expected to walk a beat on the cold stone battlements.

A fourth and fifth then said flatly that they would not risk their lives among the powers of darkness.

"Come now, men!" said the captain, who was as frightened as anybody. "We'll draw lots. I'll put all the names in a bowl — " At this moment there came a terrifying rattle of knocks from inside a cupboard.

Dick spoke to Tom, as if he did not mean to be overheard. "Thank goodness we're new recruits. They won't expect us to stand guard." But he said this quite loudly.

Twenty pairs of eyes turned his way, and a muttering began. "Why not the strangers? Let them earn their meals, for a change. Send the strangers to the gate — the strangers!"

Tom began to cry like a baby. "Not me, good sir," he clasped his hands. "I am young yet, my life is all before me. Let the ghosts plague the men that did the murders."

Harry put in, "Not me, good captain! You surely won't trust the watch to a stranger like me."

"Stuff and nonsense," said the captain. "What kind of a bandit will you make, if you can't even take your turn at the watch?" And he appointed Rinaldo, Tom and one other man for the gate, with Dick, Harry and one other man for the dungeons.

Loudly protesting, they went out into the cold night. Jocko followed, and took a few orders from Rinaldo. "Your honor is much cleverer than I expected," Jocko was kind enough to say.

Dick and Harry took their appointed position in an archway beside the door to the dungeons, the third man held the keys.

Harry offered to take down the prisoners' supper. The third man unlocked the door for him.

"Don't I need the keys to unlock the cell doors and give the prisoners their food?"

"No, no, they hold out their basins through a little slit, and you fill them with your dipper. Be off, now, and come back as soon as you can."

"Saints and angels protect me on that dark stairway!" Harry said, with a great show of terror. But down he went, and Dick occupied himself in telling ghost stories to the quaking guard.

Harry went down the slippery, evil-smelling steps and filled all the basins. He held his torch to each slit and studied the prisoners, but none of them was Colonel Gorchy.

He found a stairway leading down below the level of the river. It was wet underfoot, and cold as an ice cave, but there he found one more cell.

He raised his torch, and saw a white-haired man, coughing feebly, chained to the stone ledge that served as a bed.

Harry whispered, "Colonel Gorchy?"

The prisoner stirred. "Who is calling my name?" He was not old, he was desperately ill and wounded.

"A squire of Rinaldo di Paldo."

"Thank heaven! He brought the ransom?"

"No. He is planning to steal you away."

Gorchy said, "I am too ill to run or ride, I fear. And I am chained."

"Rinaldo will take care of that," Harry said as cheerfully as he could. He went back to his post in the archway, and the bandit locked the dungeon door. After a while he strolled casually up to the gatehouse, and told Rinaldo what he had learned.

"Go back," Rinaldo said, "and get the keys from the man on guard."

So Harry went back to his post, where Dick was swapping horrible stories with the guard. "Dick, my boy," he said briskly. "How about our bet?"

"What bet?" the guard asked.

"Oh, Dick is a fool. He has bet me half a crown he will walk completely around the castle walls alone, without a torch."

The guard said, "I wouldn't do it for a thousand crowns."

"Pooh!" said Dick. "I haven't murdered anybody. It's not I the ghosts are chasing." And off he went, whistling.

After ten minutes he had not come back. "I hope he is all right," Harry said anxiously.

"He brought it on himself," said the guard.

"Oughtn't we to go out and look for him?"

"Go if you choose. I don't choose," the guard said firmly. "It's bad enough to be out here guarding the dungeons, without prowling around the battlements looking for trouble."

Harry said with a great show of misery, "Dick is like a brother to me, and I must try to help him."

"Go, then," the guard said. "I can fight as well as the next man — but not against spooks."

Off went Harry into the darkness, and the guard stood shaking in his boots. Soon he heard weird cackling laughter. The poor guard set off scampering for the great hall. At the foot of the steps he ran into Dick and Harry staggering crabwise out of an archway. They were tied together back to back, so that they had to walk sidewise.

"Help, for pity's sake," they cried. "A witch is after us. She came swooping in on a broomstick — and she threw a long rope that whistled through the air — and lashed us together. And then off she rode over the clouds, lashing her broomstick with a switch to make it gallop faster. — Unbind us, friend. The cord burns like fire."

"Not I," the guard panted. "Those that meddle with

witches will have to untie themselves as best they can. I'm going in to the fireside."

"But if the prisoners escape you have the keys — you will be blamed."

The guard flung the bunch of keys violently at the young men's feet. "Guard them yourselves! I am too wicked a man to die." Once inside the hall, he told how with his own eyes he had seen the witch lashing Dick and Harry together. Not one of the bandits offered to go out and rescue them.

Harry whistled to Rinaldo, who ran down and quickly untied them.

Rinaldo took the keys and a torch, and picked up a good-sized stone, and hurried down into the dungeon. In a moment he was in Gorchy's cell.

"No time to talk," he said. "The little hunchback will carry you out of the castle."

He stretched Gorchy's ankle chain along the floor, and gave it a tremendous crack with the stone. Gorchy winced from the pain, but one of the links snapped, and Rinaldo twisted it free. Then he picked up the captive and carried him up the stairs to the stable.

He called to Jocko, who was waiting in the granary, "Now comes your turn."

Soon Jocko came staggering out of the stable, with a great bundle of hay over his shoulder, and went boldly to the gate.

"Hi there, guard! Open the wicket gate. I'm taking out some hay to my horse."

"Are you mad?" the guard shouted back. " — To go rambling into the mountains, with ghosts and witches on the loose? Let your nag go hungry."

"Fiddle-de-dee!" Jocko piped. "There are more ghosts and witches inside the castle than there are outside. Come, I'm not a prisoner, I'm a free peddler. I go in and out as I like."

By this time Rinaldo was back at his post in the gatehouse. "Shall I let him out?" the guard asked him doubtfully.

Rinaldo shrugged. "After all, he's no member of our band. If he disappears, Grumius won't blame us."

"Have it your own way," the guard grumbled, and unlocked the wicket gate.

Jocko stumbled through to freedom with his load. It was heavy, for it consisted of sprigs of hay, tied around the bony wasted body of Colonel Gorchy.

Rinaldo's heart was pounding with excitement. He said to Jocko in a low voice, "Wait for us in the woods beyond the second ford."

Then it pounded twice as fast, for he heard coming along the road the clatter of hoofs, the clank of arms, and the drunken shouts of Grumius and his returning raiders.

12

Tom and Rinaldo, in the gatehouse, looked blackly at each other. Gorchy was outside the castle, and they could trust Jocko to hide him from the raiders — but how were they to get away themselves?

Grumius shouted, "Open, there!" and the raiders banged with their swords because they were being kept waiting.

Rinaldo had just time to run down to the courtyard and tell the three squires to play out their parts as new recruits to the robber band. There was a chance that Gorchy's escape might not be discovered till the morning feeding time.

The gate swung open and the bandits rode in, laden with plunder. The leader sat on his huge red horse in the torchlight, and an ugly customer he was. He had a bristling beard and a thunderous scowl. His head was flat like a snake's, and when he laughed he showed fangs like a wolf.

The garrison crowded round, telling of dishes flying

through the air and of red-hot pebbles that made burning blisters where they fell.

Grumius shouted for a cup of wine, and drank it in the saddle. "Well, my wee chaps," he sneered, "I'll arrange for nursemaids to tuck you into bed from now on, and you shall be sung to sleep, so you shall! And now, who may these four rascals be?" He whirled suddenly toward Rinaldo and the squires, who gazed admiringly up at him as if he were the greatest leader in the world.

"New recruits, my lord. Spunky lads, all of them. A witch tied two of them together with a red-hot rope, but they managed to free themselves."

Grumius bared his wolf teeth and said, "How odd that for six months we have murdered right and left, and no ghost ever got on our track till these strangers dropped in. I suspect our ghosts eat three square meals a day."

Things were going badly. Rinaldo saw that Grumius was not a man to be diddled with ghost stories and yowling noises.

Rinaldo was still carrying the keys to the dungeon. The courtyard was lighted only by flickers of torchlight, and thirty men on their horses made a confusion of noise. Rinaldo edged close to Harry, and slipped him the bunch of keys. "Unlock the dungeon door," he said in a low voice, "and leave the door an inch ajar. Drop the keys down the well when you've finished with them."

When Harry had slipped back into place Rinaldo raised a great shout, and pointed dramatically to the dungeon door. "Grumius! The dungeon is unlocked."

Immediately there was a scramble. All the bandits tumbled off their horses and ran to check on their prisoners. Grumius elbowed the others out of the way and they all crowded down the slippery stairs behind him, to make sure of their precious prisoners. "More lights!" they shouted. "Torches, ho!" till the courtyard was left completely dark.

Rinaldo and his boys could have leaped on four of the bandits' horses and ridden out through the open gate. But these horses had been beaten, mistreated, and ridden half to death. The squires wanted their own good horses. They glanced at Rinaldo for orders.

"We still have a minute," he said. Shouts were coming up from the dungeons. The gang had reached the upper level and found the prisoners safely locked in their cells. But they had still to check Gorchy's cell on the lower level.

Rinaldo put his fingers to his mouth and gave a piercing whistle.

Wingfoot was standing asleep in his stall, but he woke like a flash and stalked out into the courtyard, the squires' horses behind him. They were not bridled or saddled, but each horse walked straight to his owner.

Each of the men whipped a saddle and bridle off one of the raiders' horses and clapped them on his own mount. They leaped into the saddles.

Everyone had forgotten the big watchdog. Now he whined pitifully, straining toward Rinaldo and begging to be taken along.

"I'm sorry I can't take you," Rinaldo shouted as he rode away.

The bandits had discovered by now that Gorchy was gone, and they came streaming up the dungeon stairs like a swarm of hornets, with Grumius in the lead. Suddenly the dog closed his jaws on the calf of Grumius's leg, and gave Rinaldo another two minutes for getting away.

"Hold those villains!" Grumius screamed, frantic with pain and rage.

But it took his men a minute to mount, and Rinaldo with Tom, Dick and Harry galloped off down the mountain road, with a good head start on their pursuers.

13

By the time they reached the second ford of the river, where Jocko and Gorchy were to meet them, the first pale pink of sunrise brightened the sky. They did not know where to begin looking for Jocko, who was hidden somewhere.

Beyond the ford stood a crag, with the forest sloping above it. From this mountainside the whicker of a horse came down to them. Wingfoot pricked his ears and whinnied back.

"That's Lelia," Dick said, "but how does she expect us to get up to her?"

"Wingfoot will know," Rinaldo said. And Wingfoot did.

He splashed through the rocky stream at the foot of the cliff, and began scrambling up a zigzag path where it seemed as if only a fly could walk. The other horses picked their way behind him. Tom laughed and said, "It's like riding up the steeple of a church."

They came to a grassy ledge at the top of the cliff, and

there Jocko had established Gorchy on a bed of pine boughs, with Jocko's big brown cloak to cover him. Gorchy was sleeping, like a stone image on a tomb. His face was deathly white. His wrists and ankles were covered with sores from the shackles he wore.

Just then the robber gang thundered along the road below the cliff, trying to catch Rinaldo at the next ford. "We'll sit here a while," Rinaldo said, "and let them tire their horses out with chasing."

Harry said unhappily, "We can't sit here long. There's nothing to eat."

Jocko said, "There's enough for breakfast," and took out some bread and sausage from his pack, which they shared among them. But what Gorchy needed was a roof, a warm bed and a hot meal, and a skillful surgeon. Rinaldo wanted to get him as far as the hut where Tamara was hidden.

He said to Jocko, "You can take Colonel Gorchy up behind you on the saddle — "

Jocko said, "Begging your honor's leave, I certainly will not take the old man up behind me on the saddle."

Rinaldo shouted, "What? You refuse my orders?"

"Don't shout," Jocko said coolly. "You promised me a thousand ducats to help you get Gorchy out of Castle Grumius. Well, he's out."

He pointed to Gorchy, who looked half dead. "He can't even sit a horse. I walked beside him all the way from

Castle Grumius, and held him in the saddle with my arms. Take him up on your own great ox of a horse, if you think it's so easy."

Rinaldo said, "My mission does not end till I put Gorchy back in the hands of his own people."

Jocko shrugged and said, "Well, mine ended when I carried him out of the castle on my back. I suspect you gentlemen will all end your days in the dungeons of Grumius, and I want to get back to my peddling."

Angry though he was, Rinaldo had made a bargain with Jocko. So he counted out the thousand ducats into Jocko's cap.

The clink of gold put Jocko into an obliging frame of mind. "Look, your honor, beyond that rock is a woodcutters' path that drops down into the next valley. You mustn't linger there; it's too near to Castle Grumius. But if you can carry the old man there, you'll find food and shelter."

"I'll get him there," Rinaldo vowed. "Jocko, will you sell me your big brown cloak?"

Jocko would sell anything. He took four ducats for his old cloak. "I can buy another, or steal it," he said cheerfully.

He was as inquisitive as a monkey, so he dawdled to see what Rinaldo meant to do with the cloak.

Rinaldo sent the squires to cut two long straight saplings. He laid the cloak on the ground, with the poles set parallel beside it. Then the squires gave the cloak two or three turns around the poles, to make a stretcher. They tested it with their bodies, to make sure it would hold.

Rinaldo told them to lash the tips of the two saplings to the two sides of his saddle, so that Wingfoot was dragging the stretcher along the ground. "Now," he said, "two of you are to ride behind Wingfoot, each carrying one pole of the stretcher propped against your saddlebow. First we'll practice carrying the stretcher between the three horses, and then we'll put Gorchy into it."

The strange equipage paraded up and down the little plateau, stopping and starting together and making letter-S turns, till they felt safe in putting their patient on the stretcher.

As they were about to leave they heard the bandits riding back along the road, cursing and grumbling. They were searching the ground for hoofprints, where the rescuers might have turned aside into the forest. But luckily they did not think of looking straight up the face of the cliff.

Jocko said, "I'll do you one more good turn. I'll drop in on Grumius this evening and diddle him with rumors about travelers watering their horses twenty miles to the east, and carrying a sick man through a pass in the mountains to the south. Meanwhile you will be riding west."

"I don't understand you, Jocko," Rinaldo said. "You won't work for me, but you'll risk your life to help me."

"Your honor is too respectable for me," Jocko said, "but

I can't help liking you." And off he went on Lelia, with a last flip of his hand.

The riders carried Gorchy through the forest trails; and late in the afternoon they came to a little cluster of huts, hardly big enough to be called a village.

The villagers wept with joy on welcoming Gorchy and his rescue party, but it put them in a quandary. They knew Grumius would be scouring all the valleys, and they dreaded his revenge.

The three oldest men in the village held a conference. Living in the neighborhood of Grumius had made them wise. They decided to hide the travelers in a cave outside the village. There they brought them food, blankets and dry straw to sleep on, and they sent for an old herb-woman who skillfully dressed Gorchy's wounds. When he could talk and listen Rinaldo told him his daughter Tamara was safe, and this news was better than medicine to him, so that his strength began to come back.

The old men took turns pasturing their goats near the mouth of the cave, so that they could stand guard. From time to time one of Grumius's men came scouting along the valley track and roared out questions about the fugitives — and it was wonderful how stupid these old peasants could act. One of them became stone deaf. Another could not talk in any dialect the bandit understood. And none of them had seen a stranger in their valley in the last ten years. The poor bandits rode away scratching their ears in confusion, and cursing the half-wit natives.

Meanwhile life was dull for the adventurous young squires. A drizzling winter rain fell day after day, and they huddled inside the cave matching pennies or throwing dice for lack of anything better to do.

Harry said, "If we had a horse for Colonel Gorchy we might make a push for it. He is stronger every day."

"But Grumius has stolen all the horses in this part of the country," Tom said gloomily.

Tom and Harry fell to whispering together, and then to going off for hours at a time.

One afternoon they rode back to the cave, proudly leading an old rattlebones of a horse, saddled and bridled.

"Where did you find that creature?" Rinaldo asked.

Tom said, "We borrowed him from one of Grumius's scouts who was meddling around in the valley. The worthy fellow was taking a noonday nap beside a brook, so we galloped up and borrowed his horse."

"But he will carry back the word to Grumius that we are in this valley."

"Grumius won't get that word for two days. It will take the scout at least two days to walk back over the mountains to the castle. And the peasants have no horses to lend him, because Grumius stole their horses long ago."

So Rinaldo had two days for delivering Gorchy back among his own people. "We shall have to ride slowly," he said. "We must start at sunrise tomorrow."

This was exactly what Tom and Harry had wanted. They had grown dreadfully tired of their cave.

The peasants came with presents of food to say good-by to Rinaldo, who was the hero of the countryside. A young lad guided them by secret mountain paths to the rim of the mountains, from which they could look down on the plain.

The journey was slow. Colonel Gorchy could not stay more than an hour or two in the saddle without stopping to rest.

But when on the third morning they looked out across the open plain, he pointed excitedly to a little faraway tower. "That is one of my outposts," he cried. The road lies straight, over the bridge down yonder where you see the church tower."

"Yes," said Rinaldo, "but it also lies very open. We shall be riding in plain view of Grumius's scouts."

Tom said, "We must reach the bridge before they do. If we have to fight them, we'll fight them at the bridge where the road is narrow."

"Can you make that ride, Gorchy?" Rinaldo asked.

Gorchy said, "I will keep up or drop back. There is no reason for all of you to be killed in trying to save my life."

So off they set across the plain. But Rinaldo, looking back toward the mountains, saw a horseman waving his arm to bring up the men behind him. They had been sighted.

If Rinaldo and the squires had been alone they could easily have outridden the bandits and got away. But Gorchy was a wounded man, and Gorchy's horse was a wretched beast who wheezed and stumbled and dropped behind. "Go on without me," Gorchy said feebly.

Rinaldo merely laughed. He gave Tom and Harry certain orders, and sent them riding on ahead at the full speed of their magnificent horses. He asked Dick to stay behind with him and the colonel. They could see ten or a dozen of the bandits picking their way down to the open plain, but he estimated that even Gorchy's horse could get as far as the bridge before the bandits overtook them.

Rinaldo was riding ahead of Dick and Gorchy. Some sound made him look back. Dick had his hand on Gorchy's bridle. Gorchy was reeling in the saddle, and the reins had slipped from his hands.

"Go on ahead, sir," Dick said. "I'll stay with him."

"Nonsense," Rinaldo said. He brought Wingfoot up on the other side of Gorchy's nag, and he and Dick held the almost unconscious man in the saddle while they slowly made their way toward the bridge. Behind them, in a moving cloud of dust, the bandits were screaming and beating their horses.

Tom and Harry reached the bridge ahead of the others and shouted for saws and axes. The villagers came running to help Rinaldo's men. Half a dozen of them clambered down into the gorge below the bridge, and began chopping away at a great rate.

"Don't let the bridge fall," Tom shouted. "Our friends must get over first." And he snatched an ax and went to work.

The men cut great notches in the timbers that supported the bridge. Then they tied ropes to the timbers, and stayed hidden from sight in the gorge below. They sent a little boy halfway up a tree to report on the two columns of dust that were moving toward the bridge, one close behind the other.

Rinaldo saw that Gorchy was too ill, and Gorchy's horse too slow, to reach the bridge ahead of the bandits. He dragged Gorchy across to his own saddlebow, leaving Gorchy's saddle empty. The bandits were only a hundred yards behind.

Rinaldo said to Dick, "Ride on ahead, and lead his horse with you."

Relieved of his load, Gorchy's horse galloped toward the bridge.

"Watch out!" the little boy screamed. "One at a time over the bridge."

Dick gave Gorchy's horse a cut and sent it on ahead of him. Without the weight of a rider the horse crossed safely, but the timbers shook under him. Dick's horse snorted with fright when he set foot on the unsteady bridge, but Dick pulled him down to a walk, and he tiptoed safely across.

By this time Wingfoot had carried Rinaldo and Gorchy to the bridge, and the bandits were not a hundred feet behind. Dick called out from the other side, "It won't bear your weight."

Rinaldo slipped out of the saddle, and took Gorchy

across his shoulder. "Go ahead, Wingfoot, but gently," Rinaldo told him.

As if he were walking on eggs, Wingfoot picked his way across. The bandits came tearing toward the bridge, cursing and howling, "We have them now!"

Then Rinaldo, with Gorchy in his arms, stepped out across the quivering bridge. "Run, run!" the watchers shrieked. They feared that the bandits would reach the bridge before Rinaldo was across, and that they would all crash down together into the gorge.

Rinaldo made three great, straining leaps and stood trembling on the farther side. Then he looked back.

The bandits came galloping, three abreast, Grumius with his two captains in the lead. "Pull on the ropes below, boys," Rinaldo shouted. The hoofs of the three horses hit the bridge at the same moment, the timbers made a horrible sound like a human scream as they began rending apart.

The leaders tried to halt, but the others came pelting behind them, till eight or nine of them were piled up on the wildly shaking bridge, their horses snorting and rearing.

Suddenly the bridge gave way in the middle, and funneled all these horses and riders down into the gorge below. The bridge fell on top of them.

14

The bells rang out from steeple to steeple across the plain, telling the glorious news that Grumius was killed and his band scattered. People streamed toward the village with the broken bridge, to get a sight of Rinaldo and his squires, and of Colonel Gorchy. Rinaldo put a climax to his popularity by giving a hundred of the emperor's ducats to the headman of the village for the repair of the bridge.

Rinaldo told the squires, "Tomorrow, when we have delivered the colonel to his own people, you lads can set off for the emperor's court."

"Need I go, sir?" Dick asked him.

"You'd rather not?"

"I like this country," Dick said, blushing. "I want to enter the colonel's service, and help him rebuild his castle. Sir," he said to Colonel Gorchy, "have I your permission to marry your daughter Tamara?"

Gorchy put his hand on Dick's shoulder. "You have saved my life and cared for me like a son. And so I shall tell my daughter when I find her. — Rinaldo, is it too late to start for home this evening?"

Rinaldo knew that all of them were exhausted, particularly Gorchy himself. "In the morning," he said. "These good country people are roasting an ox in our honor."

Dick said, "I could ride this evening to the woodcutter's hut, and bring back the countess to her father."

The village headman had been listening. He spoke up, "Oh, sir, the young countess is back among her people already. As soon as she heard that her father had escaped from Castle Grumius, she made her way on foot out of the forest, dressed like a peasant girl."

Then they heard shouts from the church tower. A good many of the villagers had spent the afternoon up there, watching the people streaming to the village from every direction. Now these watchers were pointing toward the west, where the sun was setting in wintry splendor.

Across the plain was coming an organized procession, with fifes, horn-players and bright banners. Children were running ahead; grownups were dancing instead of walking. Behind the dancers came a boy leading a gray mule. On the mule sat a young girl; they could see her smooth dark head, and the flame-colored skirts trailing below the saddle. It was Tamara.

Gorchy, trembling with joy, hurried into the square to greet his daughter. She left her mule and came running toward him, falling at his feet and embracing his knees, while tears streamed down her face. He raised her gently, and they clung together.

With his right arm around Tamara, Gorchy held out his left hand to Dick, who was close beside him. Dick stepped forward, holding out the broken gold piece in his palm.

Tamara picked up the fine gold chain from her neck, on which she had hung her gold piece alongside the little cross Dick had given her when she was afraid. Gorchy took their hands in his, and fitted the gold pieces together.

Three days later Rinaldo and Wingfoot set out alone for Paldo Castle. The squires had scattered, with Dick staying behind.

Rinaldo had divided what was left of the emperor's money into four parts, keeping only a few crowns. He gave the money to the three squires and to Colonel Gorchy.

Gorchy said, half joking, "The emperor probably expects you to return him the money you didn't use."

Rinaldo said, "The less I see of my emperor the better I like him. Let him find out for himself that Grumius is dead. I want to get back to Daffodil and the animals."

Wingfoot was as anxious to get home as Rinaldo was. No journey had ever seemed so long. It took ten days of riding for them to reach the village below Paldo Castle.

No one knew Rinaldo was coming, and he hoped to surprise his household. But when his villagers caught sight of Wingfoot they began shouting and waving their caps, and then they all set off toward the castle. Rinaldo rode slowly along in the midst of the crowd.

"How has everything gone?" he asked, expecting to hear that things had gone wrong while he was away.

"Splendidly, your honor." But they seemed to be holding back some joke or surprise for him. So he rode into his own courtyard.

"What on earth is that contraption?" he demanded. All the beasts were standing in a circle, but instead of looking at him they were watching the contraption, which was indeed a queer one.

Jummo the elephant was riding a seesaw — head up, rump up, head up, rump up. The seesaw was rigged by belts and pulleys to an open chest on rockers. And beside this chest was Daffodil; but she was not looking at Rinaldo.

So he and Wingfoot pushed through the circle of beasts. He said impatiently, "Can't you stop playing with that old box, and welcome me home?"

The villagers slapped their sides, as if this were the best joke in the world. Daffodil said, "That's not an old box, it's your son's cradle."

Rinaldo had never been more surprised in his life. He looked down into the box, and saw a small pink baby.

"Haven't the beasts and I taken beautiful care of him?" Daffodil asked. "The rabbits sleep in his cradle to keep him warm, and the monkeys are trying to knit sweaters."

"That's all very well," said Rinaldo, "but how about

exercise? Why do you keep him lying flat on his back? Let's see him walk. Let's hear him talk."

Daffodil laughed indulgently, and said, "Why not take him for a ride on Wingfoot, if you think he needs exercise?"

She lifted the baby gently up into Rinaldo's arms as he sat in the saddle. Rinaldo had never held a human baby, but he had held plenty of baby animals, and his little son lay safe in his arms. Rinaldo began to swell with pride. He felt prouder than the day he defeated Count Nimpimm, prouder than the day he rescued Colonel Gorchy. "All right, Wingfoot," he said. "Let's make a horseman out of this boy."

Wingfoot gave a delighted whicker, and stepped off as delicately as a bird steps. And all the animals fell in behind him for a victory parade around the courtyard of Paldo Castle.